PUFFIN BOOKS
Editor: Kaye Webb

EARTHFASTS

It was the half past eight dusk of a day at the end of summer. Two boys, Keith Heseltine and David Wix, were still out on Haw Bank, investigating something. There was a new mound of grass, and it was getting bigger. Then the ground stirred, as if someone were getting out of bed. And with the movement came the sound of drumming. David was trembling all over, and so was Keith, and then they began to make sense of it. All that had come out of the hill was a boy about their own size, with a drum.

Two hundred years before, Nellie Jack John the drummer boy had gone to explore a passage under the castle, looking for King Arthur with his sleeping knights. Now he had come out again, and time had got mixed up, so that the ancient dead giants were walking about again, and domestic pigs were transformed into dangerous wild swine.

Earthfasts is the first venture into the supernatural for William Mayne, who is already well known as one of the most original modern writers for children. His other books published in Puffins are *A Parcel of Trees, The Battlefield, No More School, Pig in the Middle* and *A Book of Giants*.

'Once in a while a book is published that makes you feel language and thought have been new-born. Such a book is *Earthfasts*' – *Growing Point*

'Rarely has the supernatural been so weird, and yet so credible' – *Guardian*

Cover

William Mayne

EARTHFASTS

PENGUIN BOOKS

Penguin Books Ltd, Harmondsworth, Middlesex, England
Penguin Books Australia Ltd, Ringwood, Victoria, Australia

—

First published by Hamish Hamilton 1966
Published in Puffin Books 1969
Reprinted 1971, 1972

—

Copyright © William Mayne, 1966

—

Made and printed in Great Britain
by C. Nicholls & Company Ltd
Set in Linotype Granjon

CONTENTS

Part One

THIS AYE NIGHT

I

IT was the half past eight dusk of a day at the end of summer, the time when the sun goes down full before man sleeps and is up again full before he wakes. It was a warm night. The setting sun pulled a coverlet of cloud over the dale as it went down behind Walker Fell.

There were hazel nuts green and fast in their leafy cups in Haw Bank, the wood below Garebrough. The nuts were still bitter with unripe milk. Blackberries hung on their barbed vines at the edge of the wood, and the warm weather bruised them into ripeness. Their readiness comes from the surrounding air, but the ripeness of nuts springs from the root of the tree.

The wood on Haw Bank occupied the hillside that was too steep for fields. Its lower edge was a wall, with a field below, and its upper edge was a cliff that rose above the small trees. Beyond the cliff was a shelf half a mile across, and then another steep bevel that rose to the crowning crag of Garebrough. Above that crag, which was a continuous Scar for miles, lay the fells that closed the south side of Vendale.

The blackberry pickers went back into the town with the dusk, carrying their baskets or milk cans or hats full of fruit. The children came down from the hillside shouting, with their blackberries eaten. They played by the edge of the town, and then went into their houses. Light began to show from windows. There was a breath of moving air, warm and sweet, falling from the hilltops and leaving on the grass of pasture and fog a large dew.

The wind blew over the town and carried out of it the sound of the church bells in the market place, where the ringers were pealing and practising. It was Friday night, and they would ring until nine o'clock.

Two boys were still out on Haw Bank, standing among the red and white of wild roses. The flowers were luminous at this higging time of day and night, on the edge of the wood facing the light north-west of the sky. They were near the roses, because one of the boys was using them as a mark to find something else.

'It's just by here,' said Keith Heseltine.

'Then walk soft,' said David Wix. 'If it's badgers you don't want to be frightening them off.'

'They weren't bothered yesterday,' said Keith. 'I was jumping about like heck, and they carried on with the noise just the same.'

Keith was looking for the place, under the edge of the wood, where he had heard a noise, and noticed something else too. A noise could be accounted for in several ways. It could be the noise of badgers. They had a digging up in the wood, where they had made underground and overground galleries, and badger motorways leading from their town into the country round. One of their underground passages might lie near the surface down here in the pasture. The noise might be caused by the humble rabbit, returning in sickly numbers after the rabbit plague. But the most likely explanation was water. Water ran underground throughout the limestone country, sinking and springing as the rock changed below it. At the moment Keith thought the noise was badgers, and David thought it was probably water, since the field they were in was called High Keld, and keld means spring.

There was more than noise, though. There was a mound in the grass, a raised place.

'Water,' said David. 'Don't you think? A geological explanation is easiest, and you must always have the easiest explanation.'

'You don't need to,' said Keith. 'You must have the simplest theory, but a theory isn't an explanation.'

'I wasn't being exact,' said David. 'And I haven't heard anything yet.'

'Look for a shadow,' said Keith. 'That'll be behind the raised place, and that's what I'm looking for.'

'It might be a tumulus,' said David. 'They're hollow, and it might be falling in on itself.'

'It might be a giant mushroom,' said Keith. 'But I saw it yesterday, and I heard it, and it's just below these two colours of roses. When I find it, shut up and listen.'

They found the raised piece of ground, the swelling in the turf. It was not the domed hill made by ants or moles. That kind of hill is raised upwards. The swelling here was not so much raised up from the surface of the field as pushed out horizontally. The upper part of it was not raised at all above the level of the field. The slope merely flattened to it, and then returned to the original angle of fall. What appeared was a ridge lying on the slope, about seven feet long and three feet wide.

'Are you sure about it?' said David.

'Sure,' said Keith. 'It wasn't here yesterday morning, and yesterday evening I saw the sun shining on it, and I came up to look.'

'You could just have noticed it for the first time,' said David. 'When the sun gets low it shows all sorts of things you never saw before.'

'Well, it wasn't only that,' said Keith. 'I would have thought that. In fact I did think that. But it was really the noise I brought you to hear. But I'll tell you what has happened. This lump is much bigger tonight. It sticks much further out of the hill.'

'Let's listen first,' said David.

The eight bells of the church sung out over them. David let the sound swing out over his head, out of his ears. He listened down into the ground. At first he heard nothing. Then he thought he heard the reiterated boom of the tenor bell echo from the Scar above Haw Bank, and he could not get the sound from his ears. He was moving his head and tuning the tenor bell out when Keith said, 'That's it,' and began to make a sound in unison with the one David was trying to avoid.

'It's the bell,' said David; but he counted the church bells, and they were eight, and this noise was nine. Something was reverberating inside the hill.

There was more than noise to it. There was a vibration in the ground. David felt it with his hands.

'It's more than it was, is that noise,' said Keith. 'And it's coming more quickly.'

'I can feel it,' said David. 'Through my hands.' He took his hands from the ground, and began to think, biting on an elastic-sided hazel-nut to help him.

Keith laid his ear on the ground. 'Got a wet lug,' he said, lifting his head. 'It's loud. It's near. Do you think we ought to dig a bit?'

'It must be water,' said David. 'It's water rocking a stone about, a boulder or something, and then it's going to break out here and be another spring. At least, it won't be another spring, because there isn't one in this field, even though it's called High Keld. This must be the High Keld itself, and it dried up and went. Now it's coming back.'

'Oh well,' said Keith. 'I'd rather have badgers.'

'Of course,' said David. 'Of course.'

They felt round the lump. With the ground raised like this there was bound to be a crack in the turf somewhere. They found several, with the grass roots still bound across them but the earth gaping for a hand's depth. David curled his fingers under a sod and pulled.

They followed the natural opening in the ground. It ran down the swelling. They went down one each side, and laid open a trench. The turf was loose, but under it the ground was firm and seemed undisturbed.

'It should be loose,' said David. 'It stands to reason.'

'Unless the water's shifted a slab of rock, and it's cracking its way out,' said Keith. 'It would be solid just under but loose round the edges.'

'Dig back,' said David. 'We can always put it all back. I mean, we're not just messing about digging holes.'

They dug and tugged a little more. Then the turf was too solid to move with bare hands. The roots in the top layer were very firm, the soil was thick and solid, and the next layer down was gravelly stone, close-packed, that turned fingernails and scratched knuckles and would not be taken out more than one fragment at a time.

'It wants a spade,' said David. 'Or a digging stick.'

'That noise has got quicker,' said Keith. 'And nearer.'

'It isn't so well insulated now,' said David. 'All that fibre in the soil must soak up sound.'

'It sounds like a drum,' said Keith.

'It does, doesn't it?' said David. 'I wonder if there's a cave? That would make it echo, if there was a rock rolling about in the bottom of a stream.'

The noise under the ground had quickened. It went on quickening, until it was no longer rather like a drum. In a few minutes it sounded as if it could not be anything else but a drum, rattling and thudding just on the surface of the hill.

Keith stood up. 'I don't like it,' he said.

'Water's still the simplest explanation,' said David. But he too stood up, because the sound was too fierce for any sort of water he could imagine.

The dusk suddenly felt chill upon them. The wind seemed to change its nature and blow wildly and in an unfriendly way. The church bells were punctuating the air with warning.

'Let's go,' said Keith. He put his hand on David's arm, to pull him away from the place.

'Don't,' said David. 'It must be water. What else could it be?'

But Keith was no longer thinking of water. His eye was searching the landscape; because all at once the surroundings were changed. The friendly wood on Haw Bank, where he had walked alone on many autumn evenings as darkness came, where he had made solitary snow huts in winter, now looked like the threatening edge of the world, a wall that should not be looked at.

And at their feet was the drumming, like the thudding of invisible cold flames. They both felt they were at the hearth of cold hell, and that the whole world was being torn at their feet.

The ground stirred. The stirring did not extend beyond the swelling in the turf. But there was movement, a lot of movement. It was as if someone were getting out of bed. And with the movement came clear drumming. They could hear the stick on the parchment. There was light, increasing light, pure and mild and bleak.

David tried to say that it was the last of the day shining on moving water, but the words would not form themselves, because his jaw was trembling. He was trembling all over, and so was Keith. They stood clinging to each other, in too much terror to move or even to fall down, and watched what they could not clearly see, and heard what they could not clearly understand.

It was not light on moving water. David found his brain was working. The light was from a little flame. The little flame came out from the hillside, and balanced in the air, and the wind bent the flame over but did not blow it out.

There was a flame, and there was the noise of the drum. The noise grew louder and faster, and settled to rumpatatump, rumpatatump, rumpatatump.

There was a shadow before their eyes, against the hill, and they could make sense of what their eyes beheld. In the dusk the little flame was brighter than they had imagined. It was not standing in the air by itself. It was being held there by a person, and that person was drumming on a side drum, and looking round, and smiling.

They had been seen. The drumming stopped. There was the sound of the wind ruffling the grass and moving in Haw Bank wood. There was the sound of the bells, being rung down now, because the practice was over. No longer were there the separate impacts of clapper on bell mouth, but the softer flushing of repeated and faster sound, coming in waves and washes and pulses, never quite dying away, never quite coming distinct.

'I wasn't so long,' said the drummer. 'But I niver found nowt. I isn't t'first in yon spot; sithee, I found you candle. Now I's thruff yon angle, and it hasn't takken so long, them bells is still dinging. It's a moy night getting. But come on, or they'll have the gate fast against us and we'll not get our piggin of ale.'

Keith gradually let go of David's arm, and David let go of Keith's shoulder. All that had come out of the hill was a boy about their own size, with a drum. He had stopped beating the drum, and began to speak to them in a thick dialect that was their own but had words in it they did not know, like 'angle' and 'moy' and 'piggin'. So they were no longer frightened, only full of the wildest sort of curiosity.

2

DARKNESS began to lie more heavily now. In a gap in the cloud overhead a star looked out, then drew the curtain on itself and went back to its empyrean concerns. The drummer boy was still solidly there, but he was less easy to see. Keith looked at David, and David was less easy to see as well, so the drummer boy was not unnaturally fading as he had unnaturally come. But where had he come from? What was he? In the first moments that he appeared, solidifying before them, he might have been a ghost; but what ghost was so full of talk and noise and wanting to be at an inn, or at the castle gate in Garebridge? Keith thought a question or two might help.

'Who are you?' he said.

'I's right,' said the boy. 'Mebbe I's dindling a bit, but not so mich.'

Keith had asked the wrong question, in a way. The boy had heard him say 'Who', and in the dialect that is the way 'How' is pronounced; and the other way round too. Keith understood what had happened, and what the boy meant, except for the word 'dindling', but he could guess it meant something like dizzy, or shaky. He asked the other question: 'How are you?'

'I thought thou would ken that,' said the boy. 'But mebbe thou isn't t'fellow thou looks in t'dark.'

'We don't know who you are,' said Keith. 'We don't know where you came from.'

As soon as he heard that, the drummer boy said he was off to look for his friends. They would be laiting of him, he said. But, he added, he didn't know where he was, and he would be glad to be told.

'Under Haw Bank wood,' said David. 'Is that where you came out of?'

'Nay,' said the drummer boy. 'I were underground, and there was two lads following above. They've mebbe missed the way, or I got too far under. I want to be back at the castle, and sharpish, because they lock us lads in, and that's where they'll be.'

'But they don't lock anyone in the castle,' said Keith. 'It's only open in the daytime.'

'Thou's not in t'infantry,' said the drummer boy. 'Tell me t'road down to t'castle. I've not been this way before.'

Keith thought they had better walk down with him, because it was not easy to direct people to a place when you are standing in the dark in the middle of a field, especially when you are not quite sure you are speaking the same language. And they did not want to lose sight of a boy who had appeared out of the ground and thought he lived in a building that had been a ruin for longer than any man could remember.

'What for did you come out of the ground like that?' said Keith.

'I were in it,' said the drummer boy. 'What for else?'

'What were you in it for?' said Keith. 'Were you dead?'

'He couldn't be,' said David.

'Would I be dead and out here?' said the drummer boy. 'I went in at the castle, along of this tale we heard. There were other two listening to the drumming as I came on. But I must have getten out of earshot, and they've gone back.'

'I don't know what you mean,' said Keith. 'What story?'

David touched Keith's arm. 'There is a story,' he said. Then he thought he did not want to mention the story he had heard, because it was too uncanny for this time of night under the dark listening edge of Haw Bank. 'I'll tell it by day,' he said.

'Is it a true story?' said Keith.

'Yes,' said David. 'It's true. I didn't think it was true before, but I do now. But I can't tell you out here. We'll go down into the town.'

'Daft-like,' said the drummer boy. 'I nobbut took a taper-end, and it didn't last so long. Then there was this candle, set there alight, so I took it and came on.'

'Don't let it blow out,' said David. 'Is it a candle? It's more white and clear than candles are.'

'Nowt else,' said the drummer, moving the stump about, and letting the light cast shadows round them.

'Let's see where you came out,' said David. 'It'll be a cave, will it?'

'It's a road in under to the castle,' said the drummer boy.

Then they looked at the place where the ground had swollen and where they had dug the turf away. Now the ground had fallen back to the original slope of the field. All that was left was the scar where the turf was laid back. David turned the sods over, and they fell back into place. The field looked undisturbed, by candlelight at least.

'It fell in after me,' said the drummer boy.

'You were lucky to get out,' said Keith.

'There's them that hasn't,' said the drummer boy. 'But I'll tell thee nowt.'

'I know what it is,' said David. Now he was certain he knew who this boy was. He was sure, but he was very frightened at the thought. Something impossible had happened; and if that had come about, then something even more impossible was behind it all. But he did not want to say out here.

'Come on,' he said. 'We'll be away.' Then he did something that was terrifying, something that he would not have asked anyone else to do for him. He knew that there could be two results of what he did. Either everything would be reasonably all right, or he would have come upon a ghost.

He put out his hand and touched the drummer boy's arm. He pinched it firmly. The drummer boy whipped off his drum, dropped the candle, turned to David, and lashed at him with his fist. His knucklebones smacked against the side of David's head.

'Give up,' said Keith. 'Give up both of you.' Then he picked up the candle, which was still burning, and the drum, and held them.

'Kings,' said David, wanting peace. 'I thought you might be a ghost.'

'Who, me?' said the drummer boy. 'I'll never make a ghost.'

'It didn't feel like it,' said David, rubbing his ear. He would rather have a sore ear, though, than have his hand go through the ghostly substance of an apparition. But no matter how real the boy was, there was something in his story that David thought he knew, and which frightened him so much that he could not ask straight out about it. He thought he would be asking about the end of the world.

They went down the field now, towards the stone wall at the edge of it. They climbed the wall, and dropped down into the next field.

'Where are you from, and what's your name?' said Keith.

'Nellie Jack John of Low Eskeleth,' said the drummer boy. He meant that his name was John, and he was the son of Jack who was the son of Nellie. Low Eskeleth is in Arkengathdale.

'You don't live so far away, then,' said Keith.

'Oh, yes, yes, yes,' said David; and the other two

looked at him in the candle light that glowed from Keith's sheltering hand.

'You'll be from down dale,' said the drummer boy, Nellie Jack John.

'Garebridge, that's all,' said Keith. 'What did you do, leaving Eskeleth?'

'Went for a soldier,' said Nellie Jack John. 'That's it. There's this lass in the town; and I'd niver get near while I came to live here. Eskeleth's too far to walk and be back by day, so I came for a drummer. And now I've been off to make ...' He did not finish what he was saying, but shook his head to show there was something he was keeping back. 'I'll car quiet,' he said. 'I don't want to pick up all my mind.' 'Pick up' means throw up. There was something he was not going to say.

'Making your fortune,' said David.

'Whisht,' said Nellie Jack John.

David was quiet. He was more and more certain of what he suspected. The trouble was that his mind did not want to believe what his sense told him. What must be true was unbelievable and what is unbelievable can't be true.

They crossed the field and came down to the road. Keith wanted to go up the road a little way to where their bicycles were, but David would not let him. He was anxious to cross the road and get into the fields the other side, and go into the town the quietest way possible, away from traffic and people.

They went through a stile and through the cows that had begun to settle for the night. There was the noise of slow jaws and the occasional cough and heave of a great recumbent flank.

'I'll bray t'drum,' said Nellie Jack John. 'Then they'll come out and meet me. I should ha' done it afore.'

'Nay,' said David, 'we've heard plenty of that.'

The church bells had sunk down now to silence, except for one of them that had not been rung down evenly. It swung two or three times gently on its own, and then was quiet. And after it was quiet there came the chimes and the nine strokes of the hour of the night.

'I were an hour in yonder,' said Nellie Jack John. 'Just after eight I went in, when we could get out of our quarters. It never felt like all of an hour.'

They came to the first houses, and there was light in the streets. Keith felt he did not want to carry the candle any further; and two inches of candle were no good to anyone. He tossed it over the wall behind a gate, without bothering to blow it out.

The drummer boy stopped, and gazed at the street light in Nunnery Wynd, the alley they had come to.

'Nowt like yon i' Low Eskeleth,' he said. 'Is ta sure we's at Garebrigg. I niver seed owt like it theer neither.'

'Come on,' said David.

'Wait a minute,' said Keith. 'Why are you dressed all different from other people?'

'What for am I dressed like this? I's a soldier, sithee. Our duds is given wi' t'job. Are they mucky? After being in yon spot.'

'Come on,' said David. 'Don't talk, Keith.'

'But wait a minute, still,' said Keith. 'It's strange.'

'I know,' said David. 'It's all strange. Don't forget how he came. But I know something else.'

Keith was used to being run by David. In fact, he thought it was right he should be, and an honour too, because David was one of the bright stars of school, good at his work, perfect at sports, and full of popular authority, but easy and friendly too. Keith himself was not too bad at things, like schoolwork, and was in the second team; but he was not noticeable, like David. Now he ran on, as David told him.

They came towards the end of the wynd. There, suddenly, the drummer boy stopped. He would have run back the way they had come, but David held him by the wrists, so that he could neither go nor hit him. The drummer boy kicked with his feet, but David dodged that. Across the end of the wynd went the square rumbling lighted side of a bus, casting light into the dark, first yellow, and then red from the tail light.

'What is't, what is't?' shouted Nellie Jack John. 'What for have you brought me here?'

'This is the way to the castle,' said David.

The drummer boy calmed down. 'What was yon?' he said. 'Did I see it?'

'It was a ...' Keith was going to say that it was a bus, but David let go of the drummer and waved a hand to stop his words. Then he ran on, taking the drummer with him.

They came out into the market place. It was empty of people. Two or three cars were parked in it, and a lorry. The church stood in the middle, and all round were dark shop windows, with here and there a neon notice over one.

'It's not like it was yesterday,' said Nellie Jack John. 'Where's all the horses?'

'Come to the castle and I'll tell you,' said David. 'You have to come.'

They crossed the market place, and turned up Castle Wynd, towards the keep. It was dark up here, except for one lamp at the corner, and in the glow of room-light behind curtains. The castle gate was in darkness, and no light showed from anywhere along the walls.

'They've never left since I went out,' said the drummer boy. 'It takes three days to move the regiment out, they said, and I was never three days in yon passage. I wouldn't live, not without a drop to eat or drink. It didn't feel like an hour, and it was just that.'

'Was it?' said David. 'How long was it?'

They went right up to the gateway. There was evening light showing through, where the sky was still light over Walker Fell. The courtyard of the castle was empty, and there were no doors, only the iron gates that stopped people and did not hinder the wind or the light. The iron gates were fast shut.

'It isn't right, this,' said the drummer boy. 'It's not.'

David led him back down the wynd a little way. 'We'll go over the fence,' he said. 'Don't speak.' He climbed the fence to one side. The drummer boy felt the invisible wire in the darkness, and climbed after him.

'I'll sound my drum,' he said. 'They'll come then.'

'Not yet,' said David. Keith followed the drummer. He did not know at all what was in David's mind. He hardly knew what was in his own.

They crossed the lawns that lay round the castle, and went right round to the east end, where the crumbled towers looked towards the next day. Here there was a way into the bailey, over the broken wall. They climbed up the fallen stones, and down on to the clipped grass of the four acre enclosure.

'Now,' said David. 'Where is everything?'

'There's nothing left,' said the drummer boy. 'I'll sound for them,' and he pulled out two sticks, and beat a roll on the drum. The echo of it travelled round the castle, and went over the edge of the rock down towards the river, and was lost in the long quietness of Vendale. There was no answer of any sort.

'What's happened?' said Nellie Jack John. 'What's come to them in an hour? Where are they all?'

3

THE whole castle wall has long since fallen, all along the edge of the rock overlooking the river. Now the mown grass comes to the edge, and there is a fence, not to keep out any strangers, but to keep in the visitors. But the rest of the walls round the great court are there still, hiding the town from the castle and the castle from the town. In places they have crumbled, or have had their stuff quarried away to make houses in the town; but there is enough to show clearly what the castle was like.

The internal buildings of the castle have mostly gone. The keep is there, hollow as a reed, and there are two more dry towers, and the skull of a dining hall. There is the stump of a well casing, and the empty socket in the ground where water once lay.

'No guns,' said Nellie Jack John. 'They're off, that's it, and I'll have to follow, and it'll be a whipping.'

'There aren't any guns,' said Keith. 'There haven't been guns here since I can remember.'

'Thou'd not ken,' said Nellie Jack John. 'It's just the soldiers get to see guns. Thou'll be out of the town and never see sike as our artillery.'

'There aren't any soldiers here now,' said Keith.

'Thou's a canny fellow,' said the drummer boy. 'That's what I've said a time or two.'

David was pacing up and down on the green grass. Keith knew he was thinking. David had a grave way with him of deliberating and then pronouncing. People would listen to him, boys and masters. He walked up and down now against the distant window of clear sky west over Walker Fell, where the last gleam looked in over Vendale. Then he stood and faced Keith and Nellie Jack John.

'What year is it?' he said.

'Forty-two,' said the drummer boy. 'What year is it wi' thee?'

'The same year as it was yesterday,' said David, before Keith could speak. 'Let's sit on this rock for a bit.'

'Nay,' said Nellie Jack John. 'I'll find my quarters and you fellows can be off. There's only soldiers in here of a night.'

'Is that where you sleep?' said David.

'Aye,' said Nellie Jack John. 'Up in yon wall. They won't let us lads sleep in a tent, because we die off so soon if we do. There was one went a bit back, and that's what they took me for, in his stead.'

They stumbled in darkness towards the tower, which was black against grey sky. There was rough ground underfoot. Though the grass was mown each week there was a great deal of low wall showing the outlines of previous buildings, uncovered by the Ministry of Works and left out for interest. It was something to see for your shilling. Keith barked his shins on one of the walls. He muttered a bit, because he did not like to swear in front of David. If David swore it sounded respectable and necessary. If anyone else swore in front of him it sounded childish and petulant and weak.

'Don't say anything,' said David, softly.

'I didn't,' said Keith, a little surprised that David should think he had sworn. Never before had he said anything for or against swearing. He had always managed to convey his disapproval just by being there, a thing that Keith sometimes resented very much, and at other times marvelled at. David had a presence with him, even when he was doing nothing.

'I don't mean swearing,' said David. 'I mean about him. I know what's happened, and I'll have to tell him in a bit.'

'What happened?' said Keith. 'What do you know? Tell me first, because I don't like being out here in the dark with a sort of ghost.'

'Wait on,' said David.

They followed Nellie Jack John. He was feeling his way up a broken stair towards the tower. David ran up beside him, to stop him when he reached the tower, because he knew that there was no sleeping place there for anyone, and no floor. There was an iron bar, and that was all, and the drop into the cellars of the tower.

Nellie Jack John came to the iron bar, and stopped. He shook the bar. 'What is it?' he said.

'Look,' said David. He brought out a match and struck it. Nellie Jack John shrank away from the sudden flame, and then looked round at what the light of it showed. There was the dark depth below, and beside him the ruined doorway with the wallflowers and herb robert rooted in the cracks of the stone. Above was the roofless tower and the gaping windows. David let the match drop into the windless cellar. The flame went blue as the little stick fell, then landed on the broken stone below, flared up and showed the walls, and then died.

After it none of them could see anything. They could hear each other's breathing, and that was all. Then their eyes could see the sky again, and then the paleness of skin, and eye could see eye.

Nellie Jack John sat down where he was and leaned against the wall.

'Where's my supper at, then?' he said. His mind was not going to believe yet. Keith felt in his pocket for the light unripe nuts he had gathered in Haw Bank. He put a handful down. Nellie Jack John picked them up and felt them.

'Nuts,' he said, and put one in his mouth between his

teeth, to crack the shell. 'Nay,' he said, spitting it out. 'That's not ready. Them's not brown-leemers.'

Brown-leemers are ripe nuts, ready to slip shining from their leafy holder and be cracked smartly and be mellow on the tongue.

'It's the time of year,' said David.

'Nay, there's niver nuts in May,' said the drummer boy. 'That's a song t'lasses sing.'

'It is yet,' said David. 'But it isn't May.'

'It was May an hour ago,' said Nellie Jack John. 'I was smelling the blossom when I went in the rock.'

He cracked a nut carefully, and chewed up the kernel. 'My mob's that dry,' he said. 'There's watter in t'cundith.'

'Water where?' said David, now that he came across an unfamiliar word.

'In t'cundith,' said the drummer boy. 'Where t'watter runs.'

'It's all dried up,' said Keith.

'We can't find it in the dark,' said David. 'Where did you go into the rock?'

'I'll not tell you that,' said the drummer boy. 'Ask on.'

David sat beside the drummer boy. 'I'll have to tell you something,' he said. 'You'd better come home with me.'

'Nay, we've to stop in this end of the night,' said the drummer boy. 'Or we'll be whipped.'

'There's nobody here to whip you,' said David.

'They'll not be so far,' said the drummer boy.

'Nellie Jack John,' said David, 'don't you think there's something different about this place now.'

'I do that,' said the drummer boy. 'It doesn't stink so much as it did.'

'And it's fallen in more, and got in a ruin.'

'It has that,' said the drummer boy.

27

'And there's no folk about. And listen.'

They listened. Keith thought there was no unusual sound. A car started in the market place, went up the steepness in a low gear, and then hurried along King Street to the roundabout and along the Reeth road.

'Wild boars,' said Nellie Jack John. 'They come up by the town of a night.'

Then there was a noise in the sky. Keith and David were used to the night flight from Liverpool to Newcastle that went winking overhead in the darkness. Tonight it was just under the cloud, the same old Dakota, lumbering over the hills, echoing over each dale in turn.

Nellie Jack John put a hand on David's arm. 'I don't like that so much,' he said. 'I don't.'

'It was May time when you went in that tunnel,' he said. 'It's September now, turning to October.' Then he told him the year.

The drummer boy looked at him. 'Nay,' he said. 'Thou's chousing me.'

'No,' said David. 'You were two hundred years and more in that passage, just walking through. I know about you. You went in there because they said that King Arthur was asleep under the castle, with his knights and his treasure.'

'I'll not tell you the spot,' said Nellie Jack John.

'But that's what you did,' said David. 'You took the drum, because you were going to play it all the way, and your friends were going to follow on the ground above, to see where the passage went. Then they would dig down and find the treasure.'

'Ay,' said Nellie Jack John. 'It were that.'

'You went in,' said David. 'They heard the drum going fro a bit, and then it stopped. And you never came out.'

28

'I niver stopped,' said Nellie Jack John. 'I played all the time, right on. And I came out.'

'You came out,' said David. 'But two hundred years later.'

'It can't be so,' said Nellie Jack John. 'It would never be. I niver heard owt like it.'

'If King Arthur can be asleep there all this time, then you can be there a long time too,' said David.

Keith could not bear this story in this place at this time of night.

'Let's go home,' he said.

'Ay,' said Nellie Jack John. 'Give up your tale, and let's be having some ale and be off to bed.'

'It's true, though,' said David. 'This is not 1742. Not seventeen anything, but nineteen something. You were two hundred years walking.'

'I thought I wanted my supper,' said Nellie Jack John. 'But two hundred years is out of all reckoning.'

'It can't be right,' said Keith.

'It's the simplest explanation,' said David. 'You told me just now that the simplest theory was the best one. Try and explain it another way.'

'Yes, but that story about King Arthur,' said Keith. 'You just made that up.'

'I didn't,' said David. 'I can show you it in a book. I thought you would know it too.'

'I never heard of it,' said Keith. 'Why would the drumming stop if he didn't stop doing it?'

'Oh, work it out,' said David. 'Nellie Jack John, you'd better come to my house tonight.'

'Nay,' said the drummer boy. 'If there's nowt here, then I's off home t'i Eskeleth.'

They all sat where they were for a time, letting the idea sink into their minds. But even David's mind, which had been playing with the idea longest, would not take it in.

It was not possible by ordinary standards of thought for a boy to walk for two hundred years underground, and then come out. Nor was it possible for two more boys to meet him and talk to him, even fight with him for a moment. There were too many impossible things. But the only explanation was the impossible one.

'I's off,' said Nellie Jack John, standing up and scattering nuts over the others. 'I'll see my lass, Kath, and she'll tell me I's right, and me and t'other fellows will give thee bounce in the morning.'

'No,' said David. 'Come back with me.'

'Nay, I will not,' said Nellie Jack John. 'There's two liars I niver want to meet again without I've a brog wi' me, and then I'll brog them. I'll fend the night by meself, and then we'll see.'

David stood up too. He was prepared to take Nellie Jack John and drag him home, rather than let him wander about in the strange night of a different century, where he would know nothing about so many things. But Nellie Jack John pulled his arm away from David's hand, and ran across the grass of the castle bailey, towards the edge of the rock, tripping and stumbling as he went. They heard his words change to a different sound. When he had come to the edge of the rock, and was casting about for a way to go down, he was no longer speaking and calling them liars and villains and claiming they were mainswearing him, but gasping out sobs. As he went down the rock, clambering and scrambling, his voice grew louder. Anger gave way to fear, and his last cry was one of terror, coming up the rock out of the darkness.

They could not find him in the dark. They climbed down the way he must have gone, and searched the walk below, in case the terror was from falling. But he was not there. Then David went home and brought out a torch, and they looked again. He was not there. In the end David said he certainly had not fallen, and went home abruptly. Keith followed.

4

It was dry morning. In the night the rising wind had swept away the dew that fell at dusk. Now the same wind was lifting dust in the street, and skittering the occasional first withered leaf from the first yellowing trees. It was not a wind that closed eyes against specks and grit, but it did cover gutter water from washed pavements with a film of particles, and it made the dogs look sideways at the corners of the houses.

David came round early to Keith's house, and let himself in at the back door. Keith was eating porridge and thinking about the night before. His memory of it had only the stability of a dream. He explained it to David, between mouthfuls.

'We've had supper, and breakfast,' said David. 'But he hasn't. We'd better find him and take him some.'

'It's unreal,' said Keith.

'Unreal but actual,' said David. 'It was just like it was. If a thing's happened it's happened.'

'It isn't reasonable,' said Keith. 'It's an effect without a cause.'

'There's plenty of them,' said David. 'But he's the most orphanist person there ever was, and nobody else knows him. So if he exists, whether he's a cause or an effect, we've still got to do something about him.'

Keith thought a bacon sandwich was the best thing to fill up a gap that had lasted all night, and prepare for a future gap too. He had bacon ready for himself next. Instead of eating it he pressed it between two thick slices of bread and looked for a cloth to wrap it in. Cloth is better than paper for wrapping warm bacon sandwiches of fairly new bread.

They took an Individual Portion of cornflakes, a bottle of milk and the bottom of a bag of sugar, a plate for the cornflakes, and a spoon. They put Keith's new potful of tea in a flask, with sugar ready in it, and a mug to drink it from, and since there is something impracticable about marmalade for outdoor meals, they took a thick piece of slab cake.

'If he's gone,' said David, 'we shall have to eat it ourselves.'

Keith thought there were worse things for them to find than that the drummer boy had merely gone. He might still be there, but beyond all breakfasts. If he were, then probably no one would eat what they had brought. He wanted to say the thought out aloud to David, but their eyes met, and he knew David had thought the same thing.

'I brought a rug,' said David. 'To sit on.'

'Or cover him,' said Keith ; and their eyes met again. So they hesitated.

'Come on,' said David. 'We'll make a fire.'

Outside the wind at first struck cool. Then it mellowed and, with the sunshine, was warm. It was still only half past eight, and the town was empty, the shops still shut. Cars were moving through, and buses were shuttling in and out of the market place, though not so many as on a schoolday. Chimney smoke blew high, and birds breasted the breeze, floating on its tide like burnt paper.

The castle gates were shut. They did not open until half past nine. It was not sensible to climb the fence as they had the night before, because the fence was in full view of the gatekeeper's windows.

'I always had the feelings the gates were only closed

when I came to them at night,' said David. 'I thought they were open all day, somehow.'

Keith looked through the open ironwork. The sward inside was clear and empty. No one lurked there.

'We'll look on the rock first, anyway,' said David. 'We don't want to be inside before it's open or they'll know we shouldn't be there.'

They went out into the market place again, down Castle Wynd. They turned left, and left again, under the castle wall where the houses were built against it, and came out on to Castle Walk. The Walk swung down the face of the rock, and round under the castle. They had come this way the night before, and shone light up on to the rock above, without finding the drummer boy.

Keith looked up, and David looked down. The rock was sheer in places, but there were many ledges and slopes, and cracks where trees grew. Upwards the eye was filled with green and gold and blue, and the silver glitter of water leaking from the rock. Downwards there was the same green and gold, the harder blue of the river, flecked like the sky with white, and the yellow of the lichen on the rooftops of the cottages by the river. Down to the east was the bridge, with a red cow standing on the far side by the water's edge, visible through one of the arches. Behind the bridge was the dark background of great trees on Ven Bank. A little way across from that were the odd hyperbolas of railway round the station.

Keith found first. There was a bright red thing on a ledge. He called David, and they went up. As they went the thing became clearer. It was not only red, but gilded too. When they came to it they found it was a hat, or cap without a peak. They knew what it was. Close beside it was a drumstick, with one end worn, and the other marked black where a hand that was not often washed had held it.

'He came this way,' said David. They quartered the ground below the find, down to the Walk again; but there was nothing else there. Then they both crossed the walk and went into the ground below.

David found the next sign. It was the other drumstick. He carried both of them and the cap.

In a bush, a hundred yards further down, lay a figure dressed in red. It was still, bare-headed, and beside it was the drum. From the drum to the bush, from the bush to the shoulder of the still figure, a late spider had spun a web.

Both boys stopped twenty feet away. Down here the dew was not lifted from the ground, and it swung in the spider's web.

'Do you think we ought to get someone?' said Keith. He saw David's throat swallow, and knew they both had the same dryness, a dryness that had to be swallowed though there was nothing there.

'I'll look,' said David, and stepped forward at once. Keith knelt down, because he felt he was not firm on his feet. When he was down he felt he might be praying, but he did not know how to pray. 'Prayer is telepathy,' he thought, 'and the human brain shows no evidence of being able to transmit any sort of signal, therefore telepathy does not exist, therefore prayer does not exist, therefore, therefore, therefore there is no receiver, no God. But I believe in God, they tell me. Oh God, don't let him be dead. Don't let David find him dead. Don't let me see him if he's dead.'

'Come on,' said David, breaking the prayer in the middle. The said half of it went winging away – where? – and Keith looked up at David.

'He's all right,' said David. 'Cold, I think, that's all.'

Nellie Jack John was so cold from a night under the sky that he did not want to move.

'I's starkened,' he said, drawing his elbows closer to himself, and speaking with a little voice. 'And starved.'

'I'll make a fire,' said David.

'And clemmed,' said John.

'We've brought something,' said Keith. He wanted to raise the boy up and comfort him, with gladness at finding him alive. Instead he helped David to gather wood and the dry bottom grass for tinder. David put a match to the kindling and the fading smoke went up.

David's face was very solemn whilst he tended the fire. Keith reckoned he had had a thought that he was not ready to say yet. He did not ask.

The drummer boy felt the heat on him soon. He raised a hand towards the flames. Then he sat up, and let the fire play on his face. 'It's better ner t'sun,' he said.

'We brought you breakfast,' said Keith.

'More of thy words,' said the drummer boy. 'Brecacus it is.'

'Thoo get it eaten,' said David.

They gave him cornflakes, with milk and sugar, and he did not know whether to eat it or drink it. In the end he drank the milk and left the flakes, because he thought they were wood, he said. He was impressed with the bacon sandwich, saying that he had hardly ever eaten white bread, and thought it had no taste when he did, and he found the bacon not strong enough. 'It's all smoky, is this you've given me,' he said, pointing to the cornflakes sogging in their bowl, and the bacon. Keith thought it was a fair estimate of cornflakes, that they were like wood-shavings, and smoky. And the bacon certainly was. He approved of the cake. It was 'as good as owt', he said. He asked what it was 'jauping in yon bottle', and was given a mug of tea. He said it was not bad, but weak.

Then he stood up. 'I's off,' he said. 'Tiv Eskeleth, and see what's going off there.'

David was still looking worried. 'You've forgotten,' he said. 'You've forgotten how long you were in the ground. It's the same as if you had been dead two hundred years. It's a long time since you went in, you know.'

'It were last night,' said John. 'I can tell a day as it passes. It's mebbe a fever on me, and I can see what's not; but it'll come off me as I gan.'

'It won't,' said David.

'I tell thee it will,' said John. 'Thou bam me no more. I's off. I's not a bairn – I's dap now, and I ken what to do.'

'I don't understand half your words,' said David. 'Do you Keith?'

'Hardly any of them,' said Keith. 'I'll write them down.' He felt in his pocket for paper and pencil. He had a pencil, and he wrote between the lines of the Individual Portion packet that had held cornflakes.

'Write on, read on, thou'll not trick me no more,' said John. 'All this is some tale of mischief, and I's off to find out myself.'

'Wait a minute,' said David. 'What did you do last night?'

'Thou knows,' said John. 'I went in yon spot.'

'Where?' said David. 'Where did you go in?'

The drummer boy looked up the rock. 'Yonder,' he said. 'I can't tell. Just under the wall it was, where there came a fall. They were off to mend it next day, today. They'll be on with it.'

'No,' said David. 'That was a long time ago. The whole wall has fallen down long since.'

'Aye, marry,' said John. 'Then I was in yon spot, and then I was with thee and thy friend. Then I came down to our Kath's house, yonder, and they put the dog on me, and I came back here, and I've slept and starved.'

David made him point out which of the cottages he had been to when he looked for Kath. John pointed to it.

David looked at him sorrowfully, because he knew that to be parted from his girl was worse than being parted from his own century.

'An old man lives there,' he said. 'With his wife. He used to drive a bus, but he's retired now. There's no Kath.'

'If I had a friend I'd have half thy words written down too,' said John. 'I's off to Eskeleth, and there I'll get wit of something. There's my father and my mother.'

'Not now, Nellie Jack John,' said David. 'What's the rest of your name?'

'Cherry,' said the drummer boy. David nodded his head, because Cherry was a well-known name in Swaledale and Arkengarthdale.

'It's two hundred years,' he said. 'And better.'

The drummer boy picked up his cap from the ground, put it on, took his drumsticks, lifted his drum, and put the strap over his shoulder. 'I's off,' he said.

'Which way will you go?' said David.

'Either,' said John. 'One on em's t'bainest road, and t'other's t'gainest road: one's short and t'other's easy. T'short one's over t'fell, and the easy one's up the dale by the river, all on t'bree side. So I'll tek that, I's on it now.'

Then he turned his back on them and walked off along the slope, down towards the stile that led to the river path.

'He doesn't believe you,' said Keith.

'He doesn't,' said David. 'And nor will anyone else. We'd best put this fire out and be off home for our bikes, and get to Eskeleth before him, or there'll be trouble up there. He'll be in a sad way when he does believe me, and if we're not careful they'll lock him up for a madman. That wouldn't be right. And I want to know about King Arthur's treasure, too.'

JOHN CHERRY had mentioned two ways to Eskeleth, or two ways to get there, at least, without naming them. The way by the river was called, at first River Walk, and it turned into Fisher Trod, and then was a pathway with no particular name, so far as anyone in Garebridge knew. It might have had local names further up the dale. This path went along the north side of the river, up Vendale, and then turned up Arkengarthdale if you were going that way. Otherwise you could stay on it and cross the hills and come out in Westmorland. That was John Cherry's bainest, or easiest, road.

His other, the gainest road, or nearest way, lay over the hill-tops, and cut off all the great angle at the confluence of the Ven and Arkengarthdale Beck, and got away from all the winding of either dale. It was called Hare Trod, and it ran from Garebridge Castle, across the Market Place, and then below Haw Bank, before turning up a green lane that led it steeply up the hillside on to the moor. There it walked the ridges, along a road marked by rock and tumulus and earthwork, to Standing Stone Rigg, where now nothing stood, and no stones were at all. To go up there now was to find only the white shorn sheep and the harebell and the admonition of grouse.

Now there was a third way. No walker would have chosen it, because it was neither bain nor gain. It was the ordinary County Council road, going up the south side of Vendale, then sending a branch up Arkengarthdale, like a capillary. It was the quickest way now, because motors are ten times as fast as walkers. And bicycles are twice as fast.

One gain, one bain, and one main.

David and Keith had fetched their bicycles, and set out for Low Eskeleth. David was becoming more and more worried about the drummer boy. He dreaded, he said, the moment when the boy truly realized in his heart and mind, that he was two hundred years out of time. That he would never see his own day again, nor parents, nor Kath, nor see as it was anything that he had ever known. And besides that awakening, which had to come, there were other things he knew nothing about, like traffic, and electric fences, and railways, and the police, who might take him into their care when they found he was a lost soul – the most lost they would ever have met.

The drummer boy led them by half an hour. David had searched his room for the Ordnance map with Gare-bridge on it. Then he had found that Eskeleth was on the next map, and he had had to look for that. When they had both, and were in the Market Place on their way, the church clock in the middle was striking half past nine.

'Nine miles to Eskeleth, seven by the river way, and five and a half over Hare Trod,' said David. 'We can't go the same way, but we ought to keep him in sight. We can go a lot faster than he can, so we can get to look-out points and keep a check on him.'

They checked first by Mark Bridge, where the two ways came very close together. It was not far out of Gare-bridge, and they had only a little time to wait before John Cherry came out of the meadows. He was marching. He had been trained to march, and he was acting in a sol-dierly way, and keeping up his left, right. He was drum-ming a little with his fingers as he came.

David and Keith stood among trees and watched him go by sixty feet away. He came to a stile, and stamp, stamp, he kept his step as he went through, and gave a little tuck on the drum, and marched on.

'All right so far,' said Keith.

'I don't know,' said David. 'Sort of keeping a good face on things, that's all. He must know it's different. He must have seen the pylons, for one thing, and seen a bus in daylight, and seen people dressed differently.'

Keith took the map and looked at it. 'He's been by Heseltine's farm,' he said. 'The two Miss Heseltines still wear black clothes like a hundred years ago, so they won't look very different.'

'But their brother has a tractor,' said David. 'That'd make him think. And young turkeys. There might not have been turkeys in his day.'

'Nor Northern Dairy Shorthorns,' said Keith. 'I wonder what he'd think to that, with them all dehorned. He won't have seen that.'

'The trouble is,' said David, 'you're like everybody else will be. You're thinking that it'll be interesting to see what he'll do when he sees unusual things. Everybody's a blooming scientist.'

'Well,' said Keith.

'Well,' said David. 'That isn't the point. He isn't a sort of rat to do experiments on. We haven't got to see what he does about things. We've got to see what they do to him. He's a person, isn't he? He's a human. He's got his own private life and his thoughts, and his feelings; and he never meant to come here. He isn't a flying saucer, exploring. He shouldn't be here at all. I don't think he can ever get back to where he came from, or find anybody he ever knew. So what we've got to do is help him to be happy now he's got here. It would be cruel to experiment with him, and wrong. When he's got used to this world, then we can ask him what it felt like at first. He isn't a rat.'

'You've said that,' said Keith.

'I know,' said David. 'It's the most important thing after saying he *is* human. He isn't a rat, so there's no excuse for observing him. He can tell us with his own mouth all the rest of his life. So stop being a scientist, and start being a person yourself, and let's try to help him.'

'I agree with you, really,' said Keith. 'Only it's easy to see the other way. That's all. It's the quickest thought.'

'It's a hire-purchase thought,' said David. 'You think of it and buy it, and pay for it all the rest of your life. Now let's find another place to watch from. We're not observing, we're a lifeboat.'

'Haul away,' said Keith.

The drummer boy was still showing his personality at Brigg End, where they watched him from the beck side, where it came down by the catrake to the bridge. He was on the far side of the water, parading solitarily through a field; and he might have been leading a regiment.

Two miles later he had slowed down. When they waited for him under Racca Scar they had to sit for almost an hour in a gateway. He came slowly now, tired, and not marching any more, and using both hands on the wall at the stiles.

Where Arkengarthdale Beck joined the Ven the two ways came together: they were the same from then on, hard going for walkers and cyclists alike, up a steep hill, too narrow for cars to pass each other.

'This is where he may get frightened,' said David. 'If he meets a cattle wagon or something. I think we'll go up and put the bicycles behind a wall, and then follow him from the other side of the wall, in case he gets into a state.'

There was no need for his worry, though, because there was no traffic on the road. They saw him come out of the fields and on to the road. He looked doubtfully at the hard surface. In his own day the road would have been a green lane, or perhaps only a mud one, and there would not have been so many walls beside it. The land had been taken in since his time on this high ground, because the Enclosure Act up here had not been until 1761.

He climbed the hill, and turned to look back over the dale. From this distance the landscape looked the same. He stood up straighter and rattled the drum.

'He'll have to realize soon,' said David. 'It'll come.'

'So far he comes and goes,' said Keith. 'At least, I suppose he sometimes wonders about it all, and sometimes thinks it's all the same, and nowadays is just a bad dream.'

'It is,' said David. 'Often. But you're not even being scientific now. You're just being sentimental, as if he were wildlife, or an underprivileged minority.'

'I think he's very privileged,' said Keith. 'I wouldn't mind going into the future. Would you?'

'I don't think it would be a good thing at all,' said David. 'And it's not likely to happen. But of course it has, once, so I can't use it for an argument.'

'If I have an opportunity,' said Keith.

'I think we'd better go to the bikes and get on ahead,' said David. 'We don't want him seeing us. We'd better go right on to Eskeleth, and see what happens there. I wonder which is his house. We'll have to see what happens.'

They went on ahead, and lodged themselves behind the chapel. The red clothed figure came up in sight of the village, and stopped to look about. The only change since his day was the chapel itself, and he looked at it once, and then at the houses. He tidied himself, sounded a rattle on the drum, and walked up to the second house.

He opened the gate, walked over the flags, patted a chintz cat on the head, and opened the house door, and went in.

Thirty seconds later he was out again, without his cap, and that followed, flying through the air.

'Out of it, you cheeky besom,' said the woman of the house. 'Coming up here out of Reeth or Garebrigg and walking in. You hikers are all the same, neither sense nor manners. If you want owt you've but to ask, and you'll get. But you don't set foot inside the door without you're asked in your turn.'

The door was closed, and the chintz cat ran away.

'Now we'll have to go down for him,' said David.

But the drummer boy was not beaten yet. He had fallen on the flags. From the cottage window the woman watched him pick himself up. When he went out of the gate she came to the door again and spoke to him, but he walked on. He went up the road a little way, and to another house. He opened the door again, but he did not walk in. He put his head in, and called. Someone spoke back to him. He pushed the door open, and went in, and closed the door behind him.

'That's it,' said Keith. 'He lives there, and he's been having us on.'

'Keith,' said David. 'I'm going to be scientific now. Did you or did you not see him come out the side of the hill last night?'

'I suppose I did,' said Keith. 'Yes, I did.'

'That wasn't usual,' said David. 'It means something different, doesn't it? He says he went in two hundred years ago. We've got to believe him, and that's all we can do.'

But Keith insisted that since he had gone into a house and seemed to know the people there, then he was known himself, and therefore belonged to this time and Eskeleth.

'We'll go and ask at the first house,' said David. 'Let's not be seen, that's all. Seen by him, I mean.'

'I've never seen him before,' said the woman, when she came to the door. 'But he had just a look on him I

43

knew, like one of the Cherrys that lived here in the old days. I've only been in this house thirty years, and next door thirty before that, and my childhood up at the top.'

'I think he lived here once,' said David; and the woman looked at him with unbelief, because the drummer boy was too young by half to have lived in her house.

'He'll have had fore-elders here,' she said. 'And that's all. That lad never lived in Eskeleth in my time.'

David pointed up the hill. 'Who lives there, please?' he said. 'That's where he went in now.'

'My uncle,' said the woman. 'He's a good age. Mebbe he's gone there and they'll trace it out between them. He doesn't ail, doesn't my uncle, and he can remember clear back eighty years.'

David thanked her, and she went back to her dusting. David came back to Keith at the side of the chapel. 'We'll have to speak to him,' he said.

The drummer boy was an hour in the house. He came out slowly, and went out of Eskeleth the way he had come, thinking.

'You follow,' said David. 'I'll go and talk to the man. We should have come straight up this morning and found out.'

The old man, and he was very old, was eating bread and cheese by the fire. David knocked and went in.

'I niver so many folk in a day,' said the old man. 'Or is ta t'first?'

'There was one before me,' said David.

'Aye,' said the old man. 'And he was kin to my grandfather's father that was brother to the lad that got himself trapped in the castle rock at Garebridge laiting treasure, a bit back, and they never found mark nor feather on him. Nellie Jack Thomas were my grandfather's father, and the lad were Nellie Jack John. And there were never an arval for him, nor priest, nor owt.'

6

DAVID came out of the cottage and shivered. The warm wind seemed chill against his skin, and all the hair on his arms and back lifted itself under his shirt, as if his skin were walking. He looked at his arm, and saw the gooseflesh making the skin rigid.

'What's the matter?' said Keith, when David caught up with him.

'I don't know,' said David. 'I believed him before, you see, but now I don't just believe, like believing two and two are four. I believe it like believing I've just had a leg cut off if I actually had. It's gone mysterious on me. No, not mysterious, mystic. It's like St John the Divine having a vision of the Revelation.'

'Are you still being scientific?' said Keith. 'Or are you upset?'

'I don't know,' said David. 'Science doesn't know everything. But I'm only feeling what he'll feel when he admits he's really here and not in 1742. So the feeling I have has its scientific use.'

'Well, explain,' said Keith.

David told Keith what he had heard in the cottage. They stood at the top of the hill and watched the drummer boy going down towards the bridge.

'I see,' said Keith, when David had finished. 'It's all secondhand to me, so I don't feel anything in particular.'

'Nothing different,' said David. 'But is he going to walk back without having anything to eat?'

'Perhaps this old uncle man gave him something,' said Keith.

David thought that was not likely, or the old man would not have just been starting his own meal. It was only half past eleven, but, country style, his dinner was at that time.

'If we hurried,' said David, 'we could get back in time to have our own dinners and catch the train to Darlington and go on to Stockton to the match, which is what I meant to do all the week.'

'Yes,' said Keith. 'And so did I. And we can't, can we?'

'No,' said David. 'For one thing, we shall have to get ahead of him and use our money to buy food for him, and for another thing, it'll probably use up all our time.'

'He's like a patient,' said Keith. 'We have to watch him.'

'He may be in a fever any minute,' said David. 'You know, we might have to get my father to him. He might get shock, or delirium, or unconsciousness, or anything.'

'Parallel hysteria,' said Keith. 'Is that right?'

'Hysterical paralysis,' said David. 'We don't know anything about what will happen to him, so there's no point in thinking of details, now or later. If he has any symptoms we'll call my father. It isn't ordinary things I'm thinking of anyway, but things like that old story. I can't remember the names of the people in it, but they looked for each other for years and years, and then when they met they became old all of a sudden, and died very quickly. I'm mostly worried about old age creeping up suddenly on him. I know it's unscientific, because he must have got into a bit of time that's different, and he hasn't aged at all. But it's what I think of.'

The drummer boy was at the bridge now, and then over it. He turned to the left, into the fields, and was out of sight. Keith and David brought their bicycles out from behind the wall and sped down the hill, looking over the wall as they went. The red-clad figure was walking by the beck, among the green trees.

46

There was a shop in the little hamlet down the road. They bought a small brown loaf, because they thought that would look most like bread to him, the smallest amount of butter they could, which was half a pound, enough cheese for three, and what they could for drinking, a bottle of Dandelion and Burdock. David thought he could still stomach it, and Keith liked it. They bought bananas and apples, and put everything into the bicycle carriers. It was not so expensive as they had feared. There would still have been enough money left for one of them to go to Stockton and the football match; but David thought he should stay, and Keith was still full of the same unscientific curiosity about what the drummer boy would think about the next strange thing he saw.

Keith and David were one side of the water, the drummer boy the other. They had to wait for him at Racca Scar, to see that he was still coming on, and then they went on to Brigg End, and crossed the water, and waited on the path.

The drummer boy crossed a stile at last, and came to them.

'Now then,' he said.

'We brought your dinner on,' said David.

'Aye, I's gant,' said the boy. 'I've had a few of nuts, and most of them was deaf yans. I got nowt iv Eskeleth.'

'You maybe wouldn't,' said David.

'A word or two, no more,' said Nellie Jack John. 'I's here out of my time.'

'It's like another country,' said David.

'You might have gone to fight in France, or somewhere,' said Keith. 'That wouldn't have been any stranger.'

'Nay, it's t'Scots,' said Nellie Jack John. 'Them's the fellows at's coming. That's what t' soldiers is here for,

47

and what they took on lads for, to be drummers and that.'

He sat down on a rock by the edge of the water, and laid his drum on the grass. David wheeled his bicycle across and laid it down. Nellie Jack John looked at the machine, and did not understand it.

'What pulls yon?' he said.

'It's to ride on,' said David.

'Aye,' said Nellie Jack John. 'It has a waller look, for a beast.'

'It's a made thing,' said David. He emptied the saddle-bag, and then lifted the bicycle up, got on to it, and rode round the meadow, and rang the bell.

'Silver, is it?' said Nellie Jack John, stroking the handle-bars.

'Nothing costly,' said David. 'We'll teach you to ride it in a bit.'

He put the bicycle down. The wheel spun. Keith put out a hand and put the brake on. The wheel stopped.

'Is it for thread?' said Nellie Jack John. 'Or owt?'

'Just to ride,' said David. He undid the little brown loaf, and handed a leaf of it to the boy, unwrapped the butter, and sliced that with his knife, and laid the slice on the bread, and then crumbled a chunk of Wensleydale cheese on top of that. The boy bit into it.

They ate their way through the loaf, through half the butter, and to the last crumb of cheese. Keith got up, dusted off a few crumbs, and brought his bicycle. In it there was the bottle of Dandelion and Burdock, the bananas and the apples, yellow ones from South Africa.

'This is something they grow in another country,' said David, breaking off a banana. 'They bring them in in ships.' He peeled the banana for Nellie Jack John, and handed it to him. Nellie Jack John took it and smelt it, and handed it back.

'Go on,' said David.

'Thoo chow first,' said Nellie Jack John. David peeled one for himself, and bit it.

'Bent candles,' said the boy, and bit his. He liked it. He had a second one. Then he had two apples. He looked at the bottle, and said he thought it was 'yal', or ale, and shook his head and disbelieved when they said it was not. The name was different, that was all, he said. They gave him the bottle, and he poured some into his mouth.

He had not expected it to be so fizzy. He belched and sneezed.

'That made me bowk,' he said; and he bowked again. He took another swig with caution, and gave the bottle to David, and they swigged at it in turn. Then they had finished.

'That's it,' said Nellie Jack John.

'There's no more,' said David.

The drummer boy felt in his pocket. He brought out a little clay pipe. In another pocket was a stump of tobacco, and in a third a pocket knife. The others watched him in surprise, because they had not expected anything so modern as smoking, until David remembered Sir Walter Ralegh, who was long before 1742.

'I'll chavel a bit off wi' t'gulley,' said Nellie Jack John, 'and then.'

But when he had filled his pipe he put it away, because, he said, there was nothing to kindle it at, since there wasn't a fire. But David had a box of matches, so there was a flame after all. Nellie Jack John lit the pipe, whilst David held the match. He took a few puffs, and handed the pipe to David. David would have said no, but he wondered about the politeness of it. He took the pipe, drew a little smoke into his mouth, and handed the hot clay thing on to Keith. Keith touched his lips with it, and gave it back to Nellie Jack John. They both refused the next round, and let the boy keep it to himself.

The pipe went out in a while, and the boy put it away. 'That's it,' he said. 'Now I'll be on my way.'

'Where to?' said David, still tasting the tobacco in his mouth. He rinsed it away with the last dribble of Dandelion and Burdock.

'Back in,' said Nellie Jack John. 'Where I came out.'

'No,' said David. 'You won't get back. The books never said you got back.'

'Nay, I can't read books,' said Nellie Jack John. 'What for should I worry what they say?'

'But we can,' said David. 'So we know what happened. You went in, and you never came out.'

'I did and all,' said the boy. 'I's here. Yon's all gab. If I go back t'same road, I's right, isn't I?'

'Stay longer,' said David. 'You might like it here.'

'There's no folk as I knows,' said Nellie Jack John. 'It's all in t'other place. This is a different spot, and my own spot's waiting. It'll have to be. Places stop where they are, sithee.' And he looked round at the evident landscape.

'I'll be off back,' he said in a little while. 'Our Kath isn't here, and I'm bound to see her again. She's a clip, and all. She was here she'd tell me what to do.'

David could not find it in himself to say again that Nellie Jack John would never see Kath again, nor be heard of again. Unless, he thought, unless he comes out again in some time that is still in the future even to us. He realized that no one could really imagine that there was a future longer than a lifetime, a future with no one in it you knew. From here and now time ahead was a hazy idea. It existed, yes, but completely without detail. Time went on, but straight into a wall. You could only look back, and not very far at that. You could not even see a day ahead. Not to be here, now, was to be dead. The only thing you could hold on to at all was the actual present.

He tried to explain something of it to Nellie Jack John, but Keith stopped him. Keith did not understand at all and Nellie Jack John never would. To Keith you could be in one time now, and tomorrow you could magically (the only way) slip back into yesterday or yesterday you could have been a century ahead and have returned. David, though, had a feeling that time machines of any sort could not work. But that thought died in him, though he knew it was right, because Nellie Jack John was a proof that time could have its changes of speed, in certain places.

He stopped trying to explain anything. He judged that he was being unscientific in trying to explain. Science observed, and then tested theories with experiment. There was no way of testing anything in his thoughts. They were all theory.

'I'll be going,' said Nellie Jack John. And he got up. They went with him, wheeling their bicycles across the fields, and lifting them over the stiles.

And then, at about half past two in the afternoon, Nellie Jack John entered the earth again, in the field under Haw Bank wood. The scar in the ground was still visible, and the turf a little laid back. Now, in the daylight, a crack could be seen, black in its depth, and no more than eight inches wide, and closing as it deepened.

'Dark,' said Nellie Jack John. They looked at the darkness with him, and it seemed a whole world of darkness, stronger than the sunlight. 'I'm arfish,' said the boy. 'Arfish of the dark.'

'Arfish?' said David. 'Frightened?'

That was what Nellie Jack John meant. David pulled the lamp off his bicycle, switched it on, and gave it to him.

He put away one drumstick, and held the lamp with one hand, and stepped into the crack in the ground. David knew he would not get in. But he did. He walked not into rock but into darkness, playing his drum. 'Follow me,' he said, and went. They heard the noise of the drum, slow at first, then faster, and followed it for six feet. And then the sound began to ripple, and then to tear at them, and then it stopped, and there was no more sound. They waited. There was silence under Haw Bank.

7

THE day seemed to be hollow, and finished. It had been full, but now it was empty. There was a sudden sag in the graph of life. The unreal and impossible drummer boy had gone, and left a still more unreal and actual world behind him. Yet it was the actual day of now. Down in the town the afternoon diesel train, that David and Keith would both have caught, if they had been going to Darlington and Stockton, barked in the station, and then went out along the line like a caterpillar. They heard its wheels slacking over the points and them jogging at the joints. It called like a cat on the curve, and went out of sight. Its rumble stayed for a while, and then died in the hills. It called once more at a farm crossing, and then was no more.

'No football,' said Keith, being as actual as he could.

'There's no anything, in a way,' said David. 'It feels very strange. It's just as if the world had vanished, not the boy. I feel as if I was reading at prayers. My voice goes on them without me. Now *I'm* going on without me, just proceeding, and nothing in the world is quite touching me.'

Keith had feelings like that too, but he did not want to

let himself know that he had them. He did not want to admit them even to David. He did not understand why. He could see that he would not want to admit them to most of the people he knew, because they would not understand either, or know what he meant. But it was strange not to want to say anything about it even to David.

'It's as if he died,' said David. And that was perhaps what Keith felt. It was as if they had killed the drummer boy, but could not be blamed by the world, only by themselves.

'I feel guilty,' he said at last. 'I don't know what of.' But when he said it it wasn't quite that. It was more as if he had experienced, say, the fall of the Roman Empire, all in the matter of a few days, and gone from the glory of government and palaces to the darkness of the succeeding ages.

'It's like winter coming all at once,' said David. 'That shut-in feeling, when the hills have that look of being closer than ever, but farther off at the same time because you can't get there through the snow or flood.'

They were still sitting in the field, close to the gap in the ground. David looked at the gap, and touched the edge. The darkness within repelled him, and he took his hand away. Keith took his bicycle, which had dynamo lighting, and pointed the lamp at the gap, lifted the back wheel, and turned the pedals. The lamp came on, and the pale yellow beam showed in the shadows. But it did not penetrate the darkness. It was swallowed up in it.

'I don't think it's natural,' he said. He put the bicycle down.

'Nothing's quite the same,' said David. 'We did our best for him. That's all.'

'You did better than me,' said Keith. 'I was wanting to make experiments all the time.'

'I don't know,' said David. 'I feel as if I'd lost my head and been hysterical in front of everybody. I feel as if I'd stood on the bank and not rescued someone who was drowning, because I couldn't swim. I don't think I did the right things, somehow.'

They sat in silence for a time. The back wheel of the bicycle spun and then stopped. Keith snapped the dynamo off the tyre and the wheel swung the other way and the bicycle settled down to its best position of rest.

'There should be a theory,' said David. And then he was silent again.

'I tell you what,' said Keith; and David had the idea at the same time. What if the boy had walked for ten minutes under the ground and come out by the castle? Or perhaps the sound of his drum might be heard? They got up and rode down the bumpy field, lifted their bicycles over the stile, and rode down into the town, down the end of the path called Hare Trod.

They crossed the Saturday afternoon market place. It lay there in that active sleep of the time of week. There were plenty of people about, shopping and gossiping, but there was no market. All the activity of this time of Saturday seemed aimless and accidental. There was no centre to hold it together. People just came to the shops, and that was all. Market days brought their own excitement, and Sundays meant there was a destination, the church, and other days were weekdays when business of one sort and another went on. Saturday afternoon was dust in a vacuum.

They went into Castle Wynd, and to the gate. It was open now, and here at least there was some sense that people were there on purpose. They had come to see the castle, and were conscious of what they were doing. David and Keith got in free, because they lived in the town, and were still at school. They walked across the grass, to the far edge, where the bailey wall had fallen, from where they could look down the rock on to the river.

They walked along the edge, looking over. Then they climbed down a little way, in spite of the notice, and looked and listened, in case Nellie Jack John began to feel his way from a crack in the rock, or to sound his drum underground.

'It wouldn't get very far through the earth, the sound of a drum,' said David. 'We should have to be at the opening of where he was, unless he was just under us and only a little way in.'

They listened on the whole face of the rock. The sunlight shifted across it as they quartered it, and the afternoon turned to evening. When they came up again to the top the sun lay level and the shadows of the walls were purple and long. The evening wind had begun to move, high up, though there was stillness in the valley.

The iron gates were shut against them, and they were locked in. But that was no problem, because the castle was no longer impregnable. There were several ways in, and more ways out, because some of them involved jumping down places that could not reasonably be climbed up.

They went out by one of the easy ways, and rode out into the market place. It was empty now, and the shops shut. The lights were glowing red round the pavement, and there was quiet again.

'I feel as if I had been away,' said Keith.

'It's just Saturday tea-time,' said David. 'And nowhere near dark yet. It'll be noisier when the pubs open.'

Since it was tea-time they went home, each to their separate houses; David off up to the top of the town, and Keith down on the road to the station.

Keith's house was an odd one. It looked blind on to

the road, with no window showing. It might have been a mere wall, if the roof had not capped it. There was a door that led into a dark passage, and at the end of the passage another door that led into the house. The house was turned away from the road and looked out over lower Vendale, over the station, and out across the Vale of York. On good days the Minster could be seen to the south-east, and the flat of the sea to the north-east, out beyond the Durham coast.

Tonight there was the haze of autumn, and the nearer lights of street and house filled the haze with a luminescence that filled the eyes.

In the house, and having tea, Keith felt that he too was a century or two away from the morning and the night before. There did not seem to be a link between the Keith and the David who had ridden up Arkengarthdale that morning and talked with a drummer boy, and the Keith who was eating bread and butter by a house window in this afternoon. David, too, would be enclosed by the walls of his house, and the doing of it. His father would be having tea and waiting for the telephone to go and call him out to another case. Keith's father's work was over for the week, and he had spent the afternoon in the garden, and his mother had been making plum jam, so there was the almondy smell of it in the house, as well as the scent of roses gathered that afternoon. There was the cat, too, lying on its back and licking its chest. It was all black and strange. Keith was far away from the morning, at times, and far away from the afternoon at others. There were two distinct modes of being going on at once inside him; and the mood he was in was caused by the first mode playing against the second.

After tea he went out, and round to David's house. David was looking with empty eyes at a Latin book. He sat there, in his own room, saying that there was no translation to '*Quis multa gracilis te puer in rosa perfusus liquidis urget ordoribus, grato, Pyrrha*', especially since the next words now held a new meaning: '*sub antro?*' Into what cave, he asked Keith, did the drummer boy go? Without his Pyrrha, his Kath?

The telephone rang. David's father went out, and the car moved away. Outside a pure blue began to fill the window, and a star that looked so new it could never have been there before, shone above a roof.

'Perhaps you were right,' said David, closing Horace's Odes. 'We should have been a bit more experimental. But you have to choose between that and being better than human if you can. There might be more like him. There were once, I read somewhere.' But he could not remember more than the feeling that he knew of a similar event somewhere in the past few hundred years.

'It might have been him again,' said Keith. 'Going in this time he might have come out later than he went in, but before coming here.'

'We would have heard,' said David. 'Wouldn't we?'

Keith thought they might not. 'If the roof fell in on us now,' he said, 'no one would hear about this time. We ought to let someone know about it. Who could we tell?'

'My father, perhaps,' said David. 'But it's not strictly a phenomenon, is it? I mean, there's nothing to show for it but what we say. There isn't a symptom.'

'No use telling mine,' said Keith. 'It wouldn't go in.'

David thought they should write down what they had done, and keep the manuscript in a safe place. 'I'll type it out,' he said. 'There's a typewriter in the surgery, and I can use that tomorrow. Then we could sign it and seal it, or whatever they do.'

Keith had heard something about oaths, which were sworn in front of a Justice of the Peace, when you said that what you had written down was the truth.

'We'll do that too,' said David. 'Begin at the begin-ning, because you heard a noise before I did.'

They began at the beginning, with the first noises that Keith had heard, gathering blackberries for jam. That was when he was alone. He had brought David along the next night. After that they pooled their memories, and made a coherent story of them.

' "We walked down to the town",' said David. 'What did we do on the way? Did he say anything? Did we see anything?'

'It was dark,' said Keith. 'Getting dark. Like now. There was his candle, but it didn't give much light.'

'I don't remember about that,' said David. 'What did he do with it? Did he put it in a pocket?'

'No,' said Keith. 'I had it. And then I chucked it away.'

'Where?' said David, getting up, and putting down the pencil he had been writing with.

'Over the wall,' said Keith. 'And it's our evidence, isn't it? It's the only piece of evidence we've got. We'd better go and get it.'

'We had,' said David. 'In those days they had tallow candles and things, and mice eat them.'

They had no torch to take with them. Keith had not come up on his bicycle, and David had only a rear light on his bicycle now. 'Our eyes will get used to it,' said David. 'When we get out of the street lights.'

From inside the house the night had been blue. Out-side it was brown dusk, because the setting sun had gone red as it sank and tinted the cloud over Walker Fell, cast-ing a furnace light over the dale.

They passed among the houses, and through the wynd, and out on to Hare Trod. Haw Bank stood dark against them, but the steep fields held the light from the sunset and cast it back at them. In fact, when they had looked, they could see the last gleam of the sun itself sitting like fire among the highest trees of the Bank, as if the inside of the hill were the fire, and the Bank itself a turf laid on to burn, with a crack in it.

'Over here, it was,' said Keith, climbing a wall and jumping down into the grass.

He found the candle at once. He did not believe it could be what he was looking for. There was something lambent in the grass, a little flame that flickered there and showed how it lay in a nest in the grass, and showed too the body of the candle that it burned from. The candle that he had thrown away the night before was still burning, and was not consumed. He picked it up, and the flame stood upright, and dew touched his hand. He laid a finger on the flame. It was a cold flame. There was no heat in it at all; and it cast very little light. It sat on the wax and glimmered. Cold sweat suddenly ran down Keith's side from his arm-pit, and he looked at David open-mouthed. David blew at the flame. It did not feel it. It did not move. It was not extinguished.

Part Two

STANDING STONES

I

THE country was suddenly suffused with autumn: the latent heat of summer was all at once available, and brought a reddening to the leaves of the trees, as if the leaves were the trees' skin, and felt the blood flow fast and warm. But it was a dying fever, because at the end of it all the same green skin would shrivel and die and fall, scale by scale to next year's mould.

The high trees were tanged first. The bold orange stripe in the rowan, and the monkey's paw of the sycamore, both straight standing trees of the high windy places, were first off the bough. Odd ones fell, and the wind rustled them along the sheep-bitten turf, and scraped them on the stone that lay scattered in the grass. The high land is full of stone that shows in the green, all through the year.

After the high hill trees, those upland willows and thorns, the low-lying beech died on the twig, and still hung there, and the fruit trees, leaving the fruit ripening, began to fall. And after perhaps two weeks the heat began to fall with the leaves: the mornings were no longer muggy, but the air was lying on its sharp side, coming edgeways through bedroom windows and spiky at street corners. There was a day when whiteness touched the roofs, and when the sun came the last of the leaves that would fall were loose, and there was a rustling all day, louder than the rustle of the coming of spring, and more spectacular. The trees that were dressed in the morning, overall in colour, were at night bare poles, standing in a sort of condensate of themselves, their own precipitate. Autumn was into its middle life.

David was trying medlars in the garden, where there was a tree grafted onto a hawthorn. The medlars themselves were still green and fresh, and useless.

'You have to let them rot,' said David. 'Then you suck out the juiciness. There isn't much to it, really. There's just a thing about having something that not many people grow. They do have their own taste, though.'

Keith felt one of the hard fruits. It had no smell now, unripe in its feathery fan of leaves, in the shelter by the garden wall where frost had not yet fallen.

It was a Saturday afternoon again, and the time was coming to talk again about things that had happened two or three weeks before. Between them there had been silence, nearly the whole of the intervening time. David had been keeping his own counsel, and Keith had not liked to jerk him at all, because that was not the way to treat David. If you did jerk him into action he would use his authority, in a defensive way, but one perfectly fair and logical, but a way that reduced the offender to a state where he could only realize his own childish folly in being so abrupt, or out of time.

Now the time was ripe. Like the medlars, there was a time to taste. Keith thought it had come. From that Saturday evening, when they had found the candle, and Keith had picked it up, to drop it later in disgust when he found its strange nature – as if it had been a maggot that suddenly wriggled between his fingers – from then on Keith had not seen the white flame and the yellow wax. David had picked the thing up, and carried it into the town, and found the yellow colour of it under a street light, and there the flame had shone white, but separate, casting no light of its own, and not receiving any, not sharing in any light round it. It had been unchanged. David had taken the candle, and said no more about it.

The other thing had not been talked about either. The

day in the life of Nellie Jack John seemed to be no longer a day in the life of David Wix and Keith Heseltine. To Keith it was something he knew about, but had hardly experienced. He did not know what David thought. It was a memory that was not properly filed, but stacked away with other oddments. There was no place for it in the store of his mind, as there is not much space for dreams. Only the empty boxes of dreams fill the shelves of that part of the mind.

'You know that candle,' said Keith. His eye was on the pulse of David's eye, to know whether he had spoken out of time.

'Yes,' said David. 'Do you want to see it?'

It had been easy. Keith had been fearful. But not, he reflected, so fearful as he had been on his last day, the very last day at his primary school, when he had been in love with Jenny Nicholson, who was leaving too, and he had thought he would never see her again, because the eye of his mind could not see so far as the next term, when they would be separated by going to different schools, in different towns. He had hung round her all day, waiting to ask the question. Then he had asked it in a very hurried whisper, would she kiss him? She had said 'Yes', with the same cheerful tone as David, not offended at all, and given him a big wet kiss on the corner of his eye. And he had never seen her again. The memory of her was lodged crooked in a complete room of his mind, and the door never quite closed on her.

David had the candle in a shed along the garden wall. He kept it in a strange way for a candle, in an earthen-ware jar with a stone on the top of it. An ordinary candle would have gone out, smothered in its own carbon dioxide, or from lack of oxygen. But the flame of this one was still erect and undimmed. On top of the stone was a thermometer. David checked the reading on it.

'It ought to be more than it is,' he said. 'But this stone is actually colder than the surrounding air. This flame gives off cold, not heat.'

Keith took the jar and looked in. The candle was as long as it had ever been. It had not changed at all. 'There'll be a time when it is warmer than its surroundings,' he said. 'If it is, then you'll have a relative supply of heat, and you could use it to drive something.'

'Yes,' said David. 'I hadn't thought of that. If you think of it as always the same heat, then there will be a time when it gives it off. But one candle power isn't much.'

'What else have you done with it, besides take its temperature?' said Keith. 'What else could you do with it?'

'Several things,' said David. 'I've put it in the jar to see whether it was getting its light from sunlight, in some way, like phosphorescence, like my watch. But I don't think it's that, because darkness makes no difference to it, and the ordinary luminosity goes fairly quickly, you know.'

'It might be radio-active,' said Keith. 'Like my old watch. It's supposed to be dangerous, radio-activity. I mean, you know it is.'

'I tried that first,' said David. 'The next day after I got it home. I've written it all up, in that account we began to make of that other thing. I tried an unexposed film on it, just wrapped in paper, and developed it. There was nothing on the film when I did. Then I tried one half wrapped in lead, to see whether it was that way round. You see, I couldn't remember whether I was wanting white for exposed, or black, so I tested it both ways. Anyway, I proved it wasn't radio-active. But I haven't proved anything else about it. I don't know what to do with it, except experiments. I've tried burning all sorts of things in it, but it doesn't react with any. It doesn't even react with pure oxygen. I even tried a drop of nitric acid. Nothing happened at all.'

They put the candle back in the jar, put the stone on top again, and the thermometer on that, and left it. It was full of all sorts of interest, but you could only say that to yourself in a patronizing way, and that didn't make the thing more useful, or more easy to investigate.

They went inside, and David brought down the book they had been writing in. Their account of the Friday night and Saturday of three weeks ago stopped at the first mention of the candle, and then went on with the experiments. All that David had gathered together after that was a list of words he had remembered that Nellie Jack John had used, and which had been unfamiliar.

'Brog,' said Keith. 'I remember brog. He said he would brog one of us, or both perhaps. I found that word again. It's what happened to the Dane who was keeping the Bridge at Stamford Bridge in 1066, a few days before the battle of Hastings. They got in this tub and floated underneath him with a spear, and he was brogged.'

'I've got that word too,' said David. 'It just means broken, but it sounds a lot better. More cracked about, I think.'

When they had finished with the word list, and put aside the recounting the events of the drummer boy's coming until another day, because there was still a shyness in them about it, they went out and brogged some coal for David's father, and then sat by the fire, playing chess by its light.

David was reading the local paper with one eye and watching for some unexpected move by Keith. Keith had a way, David thought, of cheating in his lines of thought when playing chess, and doing something not clever at all, something not in the flow of the game, something inartistic, in fact. But very awkward indeed if he did do it. So he watched, whilst Keith considered.

'Ah,' said Keith, seeing something. David thought he had seen a move he could make without being taken, rather than a move that was going to help. But before Keith made the move David's other eye had digested an odd thing in the paper.

'Listen,' he said. 'Never mind about moving that bishop. Listen.'

'I think you do it on purpose,' said Keith.

'No,' said David. 'It's just a sort of local paper build-up of something quite ordinary, and I feel like writing a letter to them about it.'

'Deliver it,' said Keith. 'Not the letter. The article.'

David bent the paper round so that red light played on it, and black shadows darted between black type of headline and column.

'JINGLE STONES MOVE,' he read. 'Reports that the seven stones standing on Jingle Moor have been shifted brought an inquiry at the Garebrough Rural District Council on Monday. Councillor E. W. Hindwell, whose land adjoins the famous stones, said that he had no knowledge of any attempt to move the stones. Councillor Johnson of Brigg End said that the stones appeared to have been moved on Saturday night after the last Council meeting (September 28th). Mr P. T. Davidson said that as far as he remembered it had been a dull and sober meeting and none of the members had any cause to go out and move stones. Councillor Dennis said it was an important matter as these stones were in a National Park, and although the Council, to his regret, had no say at all in the running and management of the National Park, they still had a vital interest in local monuments. The Clerk (Mr Siddons) said there was no way of providing a fence round the stones, which were on private land, and he believed that vandals were to blame, probably from the West Riding. Councillor Watson said his grandfather had once taken one of the Jingle Stones for a gatepost, and had not prospered after, being struck with his final illness shortly afterwards. Councillor Blunt, of West Hang, said he noticed many earthfasts ploughing this year. Picture on page 8.'

The picture showed the seven Jingle Stones that remained. They had once been a plain ring, but now they were a semicircle, because some had fallen, and others had been taken away, down the centuries. The picture was a very poor one, and worse by firelight, but David would not let Keith switch the electric light on. Firelight was all his eyes needed, he said.

'Well,' said Keith. 'Now I don't know what I was going to do with that bishop.'

'Don't worry about it,' said David. 'I'll take it. But there's something else about the Jingle Stones somewhere, not long ago, or I wouldn't be bothering to think of writing a letter to the editor. They like letters from us kids, you know. You're still a kid until you leave school, in their eyes, and they don't really believe you can read or write.'

'They don't always believe it at school,' said Keith. 'But what are you working on with that well-educated reading and writing mind?'

David had to have the light on in the end, because he was looking through the bookshelves for the report of the local antiquarian society. 'Here it is,' he said. ' "At the July meeting the Society visited the Jingle Stones and undertook the annual weeding that had lapsed in recent years." That's what I wanted. You see, they haven't been moved at all. They've been weeded.'

'Yes,' said Keith. 'But why weeded? Who would want to keep them weeded in the first place. Oh, blast, I've taken my own bishop. The colours have changed since you put the light on. I wish you had black and white instead of black and red.' David had a habit of using half a wooden set, the black part, and half an ivory set, the red part.

'We'll go up in the morning and look at the Jingle Stones,' said David.

2

It is possible to get to Eskeleth by Hare Trod, but to get there that way was to do so incidentally. Hare Trod ran from the town and up into the hills, and from it you drop down either side of the ridge. The way was made short, but not easy. The Jingle Stones were about three miles along the Trod, on a beak of the moors, sometimes called Jingle Nab, which means beak, or nose.

'The stones are there to see from,' said David. 'They had that sort of thing in those days.'

'That's some more of your loose speech,' said Keith. 'What days?'

'Shut up,' said David. 'The days when things were arranged like that. June the fifth, B.C. 4012. Is that near enough?'

'Well, I don't know either,' said Keith.

It was Sunday afternoon, and it was raining a thin intermittent rain that could be seen approaching in showers for two miles. In the town it had waited in the next street for you, or flushed one side of the market place and left the other, so that the gutters ran at the east and not at the west. As they came by Haw Bank the top of it had been hung with falling rain, and the hill above crowned with light cloud. Beyond, on the Trod, in the rising fields, the distribution of the rain could be seen. There was going to be no sudden complete mist on the moor. It was not that sort of day.

The rain would close in and dampen them, then go, leaving their cheeks wet and their hands reddened. For a little while skin would be chill in the wind that brought the rain along. Then the wet would dry, and the wind feel warm. It was a wind to keep frost away.

Hare Trod went straight up the hillside. The lie of field and wall had nothing to do with it. They lay ordered by a different convenience. Hare Trod went to the top of the hill, and that was done by taking no notice of the new intakes.

'You can tell its age,' said David. 'The land near the town was enclosed in Norse times, up to about 1100, and there are proper gates for the Trod there. It was used then for a road. You can tell they are old walls and old fields, because of the way they lie. Then up here, the bit we've just gone through, there are stiles for it. These walls were put up in the seventeenth century, or eighteenth. But the really old bit is higher up. It's a wall that isn't the edge of a field. You'll see it in a bit.'

'I have been up here,' said Keith. 'But I hadn't ever been deductive about it; only sort of inductive.'

'Yes, well,' said David, because that was the sort of thought that tended to confuse him unless he sat down to it with paper and pencil and a dictionary. 'I tell you what, I'm intelligent, but not clever, and you're clever but not intelligent, and we'll just have to make the best of it.'

'I'll think about it,' said Keith.

They kept their breath then, because the Trod was intractably steep just here, going up the talus slope to the bottom of a scar, and then through a break in the scar, before lying on a short plateau. The altitude was about 1200 feet. Below them, the way they had come, the town was laid out, castle and houses, on the arteries of the valley. The brow of Haw Bank hung above to one side, and far off was the Wold country and the North York Moors, the Cleveland and Howardian Hills with their white cliffs and plantations; and all tufted with the same cloud and drizzle. Ahead, uphill, there was another horizontal ridge, and above that the sky. But they knew that when they came to the top of the ridge there would be another, and another, before they came to the flat-iron of the hilltop.

It was on the last ridge, where the fields had changed to moor and heather was purple underfoot and grouse went off like lawnmowers to right and left, and water ran overground and underground on either side, that they came to the ancient wall.

It was not a high wall. It was not a field wall, by any means. It was a heap, in places, of large boulders; and in other places only a line of them. Hare Trod ran alongside it, first on one side, and then on the other. It was the wall that changed sides, not the Trod. The wall stepped a full six feet to the right to let the path through.

'You see,' said David. 'This is a Neolithic wall, a tribal boundary. And this path was there before it was. So it's older than old. It was old when things began to be prehistoric.'

Another mile, and the Jingle Stones were in sight, lonely in their half-circle on the end of the hill. A drizzle cloud washed them as Keith and David approached, and then went on its way, leaving blue sky and sunshine overhead. The sunshine glittered on the stones.

Keith ran ahead and touched the stones first. It was child's talk that the first of the party there could wish. But as you get older it is harder to know what to wish: a lot of wishing seems only selfish. He wished that things would not be too different in the end, and then walked round all the stones against the sun, because that was the proper way to go in such cases.

'Careful,' said David. 'It might come true.'

'It might,' said Keith. 'It was one of those vague wishes, that's all.'

'Let's see whether they've moved much,' said David. They stood among the stones, all seven of them. Each of them was about nine feet tall, dark and wet today. On a dry day they were still dark. Hare Trod ran straight up to them, and then went round them on a little ridge, and continued again in a straight line northwards.

'They're older than it,' said David. 'At least, it's reasonable to think so. The Trod came to the stones, not the other way round.'

'I wonder,' said Keith. 'They were brought here, weren't they? They didn't walk.'

'Or did they?' said David. 'That's what we've come to find out.'

They looked at the stones. They looked at the ground. There was some alteration in that. The stones themselves seemed much the same.

'I can't tell whether they've moved in relation to each other,' said David. 'I haven't even a picture of them. And I can't tell how the Society weeded anything, because there isn't anything to weed. It's all plain grass round them, eaten like a lawn by the sheep.'

'But better than a lawn,' said Keith.

'Much better,' said David. 'But weeds don't have a chance to grow.'

'I tell you what,' said Keith, when he had looked round a bit. 'They've not weeded anything, but just taken the turf right out. But they haven't done it near the stones, but just beside.'

David looked and found the places Keith had seen. Making another half circle a little different from the half

73

circle of the stones, but crossing it, there were patches where the turf had been taken up entirely, leaving the fibry earth, where green was showing again. There was a little heap, away to one side, and still green, where the turf had been put. There was a relationship between the patches and the stones. A yard away from the thickest stone was the biggest patch, having nearly the same size at ground level, and the same shape. All the patches were slightly bigger than the stones they seemed to belong to. But each one had the shape of the neighbouring stone.

'It's just as if they had weeded, or unturfed them,' said Keith, 'and then the stones had moved. Some joker's done it on purpose.' He had to think that.

Another shower drifted over them. They squatted in the shelter of the biggest stone until it had gone. They squatted silently, because the only thought that each of them had was that the stones had moved a yard in the last month.

'An inch a day,' said David, getting up and letting a pool of water run off his sleeve.

'No,' said Keith. 'How?'

There was more evidence. Between each bare patch and the related stone there was a furrow in the grass. The ground was soft under the grass, and the grass had parted and joined again. The ground was more than soft, it was almost fluid with sandiness, and sand like that was not quite the natural state of things. David drew back the grass, shook roots from his fingers, and scooped the sand up. He could dig down as if he were at the seaside, with the sand getting denser and damper, but still remaining sand. There were no small stones in it, only the fine powder. His hand, which had been wet, came out with its ridges and whorls of skin, its life lines and fingerprints, marked with dust, and dust is not an ordinary constituent of the kind of sand found in these hills. The sand here was water-washed, sharp, clean, and always along the edges of the becks and gutters.

At the other side of the stones there was a sort of bow-wave in the ground, where the turf was lifted a little. It was exactly as if the stones were moving slowly. And not downhill, quite, but along the hill. Along Hare Trod, which ran here up the brow of the nab, with the ground falling to either side.

'It's strange,' said David. 'It wasn't the Council's vandals from the West Riding that did this. It's more earthquakish.'

'Earthfasts,' said Keith. 'They rise in ploughed land.'

'That's the soil that moves,' said David. 'This is the stones. You could almost say it was proved.'

'We could just say it looks as if it was proved,' said Keith. 'I don't want it proved.'

'Nor do I,' said David, laughing. He had proved it well enough, though, and he didn't care for it. Moving stones were not quite canny.

'We'll go back,' he said. 'The paper's right for once. But I bet no one comes up here to see, except us. We should have brought a camera.'

Keith was going to move away with David. But he began to look at the rocks instead. 'You know,' he said, 'they're cracked. You can see cracks in them. And there's a line round them too, as if they'd risen up out of the ground as well as going along.'

David found the cracks when they were pointed out to him. 'Frost,' he said. 'They can't last for ever. It's frost, or either they've been brogged.'

But brogged or frosted, the cracks were there, and Keith reckoned that if the cracks opened up there would be a human outline, buried to its knees in the ground. A human twelve feet tall. David said it would not be surprising if the stones had been carved sometime, and that was all that was left. He thought they might be representations of ancient heroes, or the days of the week, since there were seven. Keith reminded him of the one that had been taken for a gatepost, and that the circle was not complete as it stood.

'I wonder if the others are moving,' said David. And then they began to walk down Hare Trod towards the town again.

There was a better view going down. It was very different this way, because things that had not appeared at all on the way up showed going back. There was a farm to the right, in a fold of the moor, and down to the left another one.

'Ancient settlements,' said David. 'You can see the field patterns just round them. We can look on the map for their names. They'll be old ones.'

'Hare Trod runs just between them,' said Keith. 'Is that significant?'

'I don't know,' said David, looking either way. 'It's. . . .' Then he stopped speaking, and grabbed at Keith's arm, with his fingers scrabbling. It was very unlike David to touch anyone else. Keith stopped walking and turned to see what was the matter with him.

David was staring out over the folded fellside, down towards the river Ven. The river was out of sight, but the wrinkled hill went down to it, and up beyond the other side. It was to the other side that David was looking, a good two miles away, across clear air, and bright sunshine. The drizzle had gone away from that side of the valley, and there was no obstruction to vision.

Something moved on the far hill, on the bare moor. There was a man walking. But you cannot see a man walking and striding like that two miles away. This man was getting on for twenty feet tall, and he was pacing twenty to the full stride. And he was walking along the hill, away from them.

Keith moved his head. He was sure there was an optical illusion. The man must be on a much nearer ridge whose colour and perspective ran into the distant hillside. But it was not so. The giant walked over the crest of the hill, and went out of sight.

David's grip relaxed. 'Seeing things,' he said, and turned to Keith to hear that he had seen nothing. David would have preferred hallucination to real giants.

'No,' said Keith. 'It was real. I saw it too.'

3

THE day's events were not over. Keith and David went on walking down Hare Trod, rather fast. An extreme nervousness had overcome them both. It was not pure nervousness, but a sort of thin terror; something that went round inside them like some yellow acid, touching tender membranes and making inward parts recoil and tremble.

They looked behind them, not particularly to see the Jingle Stones again, but part of a wary look at the whole landscape. But it was the Jingle Stones that caught their eyes. The stones were erect on the skyline when they looked. Now that they had just seen a giant, they thought they saw seven more. The stones stood as if they had been playing the game called Grandmother's Footsteps, or Creepmouse, when the person who is on looks away and turns suddenly towards the rest who are creeping up, and sends back to the start those he has seen move.

'Go back, all of you Jingle Stones,' said David. But the humour of it was too near the actuality, and the words died away on his lips. The Jingle Stones looked as if they were following.

'Go on,' said Keith. 'I don't like it here.'

'Nor do I,' said David; and they both ran, until the Jingle Stones had to be out of sight. Then they looked back, and the stones were out of sight.

'It was a narrow escape from inanimate objects,' said David. 'I was frightened.'

'The Jingle Stones bit was imagination,' said Keith. 'But the other wasn't. What we saw on the other hill.'

'I know,' said David. 'But real things are easier to forget. I think we'd better go home.'

Hare Trod led them down into the fields again, off the open moor, and then along the lower slopes towards the town. There was a little patch of trees by the path, making a hedge beside it instead of a wall, and casting some shadow. A drizzle cloud came over them at that place, and made the shadow more indistinct still. They hesitated, and then looked at each other.

'We aren't afraid of the dark, in broad daylight,' said David, turning up his coat collar. 'Come on.'

They were half-way along the patch of trees when they heard noise, a snuffling breathing, and with the breathing there was the sound of undergrowth and underwood cracking and crumbling. Something was in the wood, and by the sound of it something big. Both boys stopped. They had to, because their feet could not be lifted from the ground. Their muscles had tightened in some way that took all mobility from them. They were paralysed as if they were in a dream. Their breath, which was coming quickly in any case from the running they had done, began to come in frantic spasms because their breathing muscles too were locked in panic.

In the wood the noise continued. Something seemed to be floundering amongst the trees, and breathing like a monster. There was a flash of white down among the trunks of the trees, and a tide of movement. It looked as if foaming water were rising out of the ground.

Then there was an unmistakable noise, and the moving whiteness came to the edge of the wood, and crossed on to the path. It was not one big object, but twenty smaller ones: white and yellow hounds intent on following something. They had slowed in the wood and cast around, and now were leading on.

'It's the hunt,' said Keith.

'On Sunday?' said David. 'But it's the hounds. I wonder who's with them?'

There was no one with them. The hounds were out alone. Their keeper was not there, nor the huntsman, nor any followers. The hounds lifted their heads and acknowledged the boys, and then went on across the field, following a slow trail with some difficulty.

'They shouldn't be out,' said David. 'What shall we do?'

'I don't mind going with them,' said Keith. 'They're company. But I wonder what they're following.'

'A hare,' said David. 'But not because it's Hare Trod. That's not the same kind of hare at all.'

'They'll have got out,' said Keith. 'They'll end up in a hen run, or something. We'd better try to call them off, or we don't know what will happen.'

David had some idea of tying them all with his tie, but the hound he tried to arrest was not interested, and went on without doing more than turning its head and grinning goodnaturedly. The tie slipped from its shoulders.

'I don't think they're attending,' said David.

They followed instead. Keith thought they might be able to run ahead and lock up hens, rescue cats, and, if they came to a road, signal to traffic to slow down. But just now the hounds were in charge.

There came again the revealing noise they had heard in the wood. One of the hounds had found a firm scent, and gave voice. The others followed, and the pack began to run.

'Oh no, don't,' said Keith. He was still suffering from the reflex pain of the earlier running and the heart-stopping fear by the wood.

'Things are a bit strange today,' said David. 'We'd better follow if we can. I don't see anyone coming with them, so we're bound to.'

The pack crossed the field, swarmed over a wall, and came down to a beck. The trail they followed crossed the beck, and the hounds crossed too, leaving the water muddied and the far bank wet, shaking themselves as they ran. David and Keith went to one side and crossed the stepping stones.

The sun came out again. There was the smell of wet dog, both their damp coats and their breath. Then they went out of sunlight, not because of a cloud, but because of the shadow of the hill. The hunt turned quietly towards the town, and then began to run at full pace along the hill-side, under Haw Bank. It broke out into sunlight again, and went rustling along the edge of the wood, calling in hound voices.

The boys jogged along behind, unable to do anything but follow. 'They'll be getting to that place,' said Keith. 'Just along here.'

'Won't be a hare in that,' said David.

But the hounds were not following a hare. They were following something unknown; and the place they followed it to was the place where the drummer boy had come out and gone in again.

The place itself was smothered in dogs when Keith and David reached it. They were trying to get into the ground, but the way in was too small.

Keith recognized the place by the shape of Haw Bank above it. David pulled two hounds back and saw the ground below them. It was the same crack in the grass, pawed and scraped now by the hounds, but certainly the same place. But there was a difference in the surroundings. Before, the open field had surrounded the gap, with the sloping grass all round, and nothing else to the walls. But now there was a rock just to one side, a fresh rock, with grass on top, because there was a turf there, and earthy sides. A rock standing six or seven feet high, and as many deep, and eighteen inches across, brother to those of the Jingle Stones, but new, unweathered, only touched a little by the recent drizzle.

'That's come up,' said Keith. 'It never rolled down out of the Bank, not with that sod on top of it.'

'I was going to say I'd stay whilst you went for the huntsman,' said David. 'But I don't want to now. I don't like these moving rocks. It's against nature. I can understand time being changed, because no one knows about time yet. But we know rocks don't move about like that. And I don't know what's in the wood any more. You know what we saw on the hill.'

'I'm not staying either,' said Keith. 'So forget it. But the hounds aren't frightened, and they would notice things like, well, supernatural things.'

The dogs were not concerned with anything their noses had not told them of. They were trying to get into the ground, but there were too many of them.

'What they usually do is whip them off,' said David. 'And then they have a little dog to go down and bring the fox out.'

'Yes,' said Keith. 'That's what it is. A fox. They smell very strong, don't they?'

'I never smelt one,' said David. 'All I can smell now is the hounds. Do you think we should leave them?'

'Yes,' said Keith. 'We'll tell the huntsman, and leave it to him. I think I want to go away from here. It's teatime.'

Then the hounds paused in their digging, and fell silent. They stepped back from the hole in the field, and looked about, uneasily, with the white parts of their eyes showing. But still they were very close to the hole, because a dog's backward pace is only six inches, and their interest was still in the ground.

Then there was a sudden confusion. There was no noise except for a few yelps, but the whole pack was suddenly shaken and thrown about and knocked off its feet, so that the hounds were clambering up from the ground they had fallen down to, and found that all they had managed to do was fall over to the other side. Keith and David felt the ground vibrate, gently.

Then the hounds picked themselves up, and gathered together, looking all in one direction. It was towards David and Keith, and it was not a friendly look. Though it was towards the boys it was not at them the hounds were staring. They seemed to see something that neither Keith nor David could see at all. The hounds moved unhappily, and spread a little, retreating pace by pace, silently. The line of them spread out, and David could tell from the two hounds that were farthest apart that they were looking at a particular location, between him and them. But they were not looking at the ground; they were looking slightly above it, at something three or four feet tall. Because they had been looking at that height they had looked into Keith's and David's eyes before, though at something between them.

There was nothing four feet high in the field between hounds and boys.

But there was a flattening in the grass. The flattening began to spread, towards the hounds. The hounds stood

82

and looked, and then they turned and ran, fanning out as they went; and the flattening in the grass moved after them. Near at hand it was not easy to see, but as it moved over the fog, the grass that grows after the hay has been taken, its path was quite clear, where the underneath of the grass turned silver against the green.

There was nothing left but the scrabbled ground, and two or three marks where the hounds had sniffed the rock and then wet it.

'I'm off,' said David. He tried to sound as if he were going only because tea was ready. Keith tried to speak, but no words came. His voice was no more obvious than the invisible thing in the field.

They left by the way they had come, going away from the town. They did not tell each other why. It was because the hounds had run towards the town, and whatever had followed them would be in that part of the field.

David started by looking round at everything. Then he seemed to think it was hopeless to foresee at all, and walked on with his eyes on the ground.

When they came into the town the hounds were there before them, wandering about in ones and twos, taking no notice of people or cars or buses. Whatever they had run from was no longer near enough to frighten them, and they were taking their ease, and looking at the town dogs like gentlemen and dandies.

The huntsman came up in the kennels van and jumped out, talking to the kennel man, who looked small and ashamed and obediently helpful. The bell ringers looked at them as they crossed the market place.

'I've had enough of them,' said David. 'Let's go to my house and have tea.'

Keith felt safer in the town, where he knew all the horizons. But he only felt safer because he knew where he was and where he would run if anything happened; if the earth quaked, or a giant appeared, or a stone no longer stood but walked.

The first note of the church bells skimmed overhead like a flying saucer. A hound stood on its hind legs and looked in the Co-op window, then got down again and walked round the corner.

'They'll be hours with that lot,' said David. 'I'd better put my tie on again. Then, when we've had tea we'll write down everything that's happened, and get that newspaper cutting, and see whether I can write a letter to the paper, because we didn't get anything proved up there at all, except that it was right. But I think there must be some connexion between Nellie Jack John and what's going on up there.'

'It might get clearer if we write it down,' said Keith. 'Or it might get worse.'

'I'm wondering what it's all about,' said David. 'Not prophesying, but wondering what causes all these effects.'

4

NORMAL life came back after tea, with the curtains drawn and the fire glowing. David and Keith and David's father, Dr Wix, played a sort of three-handed chess, with the three chess sets in the house, one plastic, one wood, and one ivory. Today they played with complete sets, not the midnight colours of red and black, and all against all.

Keith always found it a very tense thing to do. He ought, in theory, he thought, be able to do the same moves on both the boards he was concerned with, and win on one and lose on the other, which was fair. But chess was not like that, and his plans soon had to vary, and he went on haphazardly.

In the middle of the game the telephone rang. Dr Wix went to it and answered. They could hear his voice answering in the reluctant way a doctor begins on a Sunday evening. But by the end of the conversation he was interested and in a hurry. He banged the telephone down, pulled on his coat, picked up his bag; and then they heard the car leave.

'He's lost,' said Keith.

'I bet it's twins,' said David. 'It's usually a Sunday job.'

'One black and one white,' said Keith. 'Black with his right hand and white with his left.'

'One plastic and one ivory,' said David. 'But we'll finish our game and see what he says when he comes in.'

Dr Wix was gone nearly an hour. He came in disinclined to finish the games he had begun. Instead he stood by the fire warming his legs, and drinking whisky.

David nodded his head to Keith, to signify that they should go to David's room and leave Dr Wix to get over his tiredness or anger at an unreasonable patient.

'Don't go,' said Dr Wix. 'Something rather interesting came up. I think I can tell you about it, but it's not for general consumption.'

'Triplets,' said David.

'No,' said Dr Wix. 'Much stranger. That call was to Swang, you know where that is.'

'Just up the hill,' said David. 'The farm just about next to the Jingle Stones.'

Dr Wix nodded. 'Frank Watson rang up. It's his farm; in fact it's been in the family for generations. You'll know him, he's the district councillor for his parish.'

'Big red man,' said Keith. 'He's a distant cousin of my mother.'

'Like most people,' said Dr Wix. 'His wife was in a distressed state. He'd found her when he came in from

85

milking, lying on the floor, furniture overturned, the fire out, soot on the hearth, the kettle on its side. The first thing he noticed was the cat, up on a shelf, terrified out of its wits. He couldn't get near it. But he didn't tell me all that on the telephone. He just asked me to come at once and see what had happened to Mrs Watson, whilst he looked round the house. I wondered what had happened, so I called at the police station on the way and took up the constable. I didn't know what I'd find. When we got there the lights were on in every room in the house, and in the shippon, and Watson had the car head-lamps and the tractor lamps on too, and a lantern lit in the garden. Mrs Watson had recovered a bit, and we soon found out there was no need of the constable. I thought she might have been attacked and robbed, but there was nothing missing. She said she was sitting by the fire knitting, because she doesn't mind knitting on a Sunday any more, though she wouldn't have done it when she was a girl. Suddenly the cat jumped on the shelf and seemed to have a sort of fit. It was hissing and growling and claw-ing at the air, and she said it got up to twice its size and began knocking things off. She went to pick things up, and there was noise like something running over the ceil-ing. She looked round, thinking there was something there. She said she almost saw the thing. The next thing she knew was that the kettle was off the trivet in the fen-der and on its side on the fire, and the fire was spitting itself on to the hearthrug and smelling like Hell. She wasn't swearing; she thought Hell would smell like that. Then the table shifted itself half round, and the things on it stayed where they were, so that half of them fell down on to the floor. Her knitting needles sprang across the room, the hearthrug whisked itself away from the fire-place. She was standing on one end of it, and she remem-bers falling when it was pulled from under her, and a noise as if something was whirling round the room knocking things over. Then she found her husband bending over her, and a little while later the constable and I came in. Watson himself had found her, rung me up, and then gone round the rest of the house, because he heard something. He had taken his shot-gun with him, and I don't blame him. He didn't see anything, but he left all the lights on. Then he went outside, and heard things there. He said that stones from the tops of walls were rolling about the yard and the garden, and something was in the shippon upsetting the cows. Whatever it was had lifted the milk-cooler out of the milk kit and dropped the hose in, so that the kit was filling with water. He turned that off, and left lights on, switched on the tractor and car lights, and put two lanterns on in the garden. By the time we got there all was quiet again. The cat had settled down and was licking its chest, and was quite friendly. Mrs Watson was shocked, but not hurt. I gave her a sedative and she went to bed. Then we looked at the cat. It was unharmed, and perfectly friendly. Watson tipped some milk into a saucer for it, and went to get it. Then it had another fit, as soon as it put its nose to it. It wasn't a convulsion. It was just as if something had attacked it, and it began to defend itself. It ran away from the milk, back on to the shelf, watching something. We watched the cat. And when we turned round and looked at the milk, by accident really, because there didn't seem to be any clinical significance in the milk itself, we found it had gone. Watson blinked. The constable thought one of the dogs might have come in and lapped it up; but that wasn't possible, because the doors were closed. Something had drunk it, though. Then Watson calmed down all at once, and said there was nothing to worry about. He said he knew what it was, and he's heard of it before.'

'What?' said David. He and Keith had been looking at each other during the story, because there was something familiar about it. Something invisible had been moving.

'He said it was the boggart,' said Dr Wix. 'And I must say that it fills all the conditions. Boggarts are slightly touchy house spirits, with a taste for milk and other little gifts, and they don't greatly care for cats and dogs. There used to be a lot of stories about them. You'll know the famous one, where this family had been so badly plagued by a boggart that they decided to leave. Now, they had to do this suddenly and in silence, so that the boggart wouldn't find out. So one day they took everything out of the house and loaded it on to a cart. Just as they were off a neighbour came by and said: "You're off, then?" "Aye," says the boggart, looking out of the luggage on the cart. "We're flitting."'

'And that was that, I suppose,' said David. 'Have they always had a boggart at Swang?'

'They used to have,' said Dr Wix, 'from what Frank Watson said. And now it's come back to plague them.'

'I hope it's stayed there,' said David. 'We don't want it here.'

'Maybe not,' said Dr Wix. 'But my clinical eye noticed that you and Keith had some knowledge between you as I was telling you about the Swang boggart. What do you know?'

'Something similar,' said David. 'Shall we tell you?'

'In a minute,' said Dr Wix. 'I haven't quite finished. When the constable and I left we found that a stone gatepost had fallen from its place at the entrance to the farm, and was blocking the lane completely. Watson himself shook his head. He said he wasn't a superstitious man, but he knew something about that gatepost. He said he believed it was one of the Jingle Stones, brought there by his grandfather, who had died rather suddenly after bringing it down from the top of the hill. He said he would put it back, in daylight. But it was more than he could do, or his tractor could, to move it then. We had to drive through his home field and out into the lane lower down to get back. The thing that beats me is how calm he was about it all. But I suppose it isn't superstitious to believe in something you can actually see happening and experience. But what about your story?'

David began to recount what they had seen that afternoon. Keith was embarrassed in case he mentioned the giant they had seen on the far hill; but David said nothing about that. He only talked about the Jingle Stones and the place the hounds had led them to, without saying why they knew the place already. He described what the hounds had done, and what they seemed to have seen.

'We have six reliable witnesses,' said Dr Wix. 'But I think they would all be well advised to say nothing about their testimony until they know what it's all about. I can't think of a natural explanation that agrees with known scientific facts. So I'm not going to say a thing. But just get that paper, and I'll read what the Council said about the Jingle Stones. Was Councillor Watson among them, I wonder?'

'Somebody mentioned a gatepost,' said David.

Dr Wix read the paper. 'It doesn't add up,' he said. 'Now I think I will finish those chess games.'

He lost them both.

Keith went home through the late Sunday evening streets, anxious at every shadow. But everything was quiet. He thought he caught a glimpse of a hound, once, and called to it, but it wandered away. He thought it would go home when it felt hungry again. He went to bed, and whilst he was listening in case a boggart moved in the roof or under the floor, he fell asleep.

In the morning, at school, there was no rumour of visitations and boggarts. The only story was that the hounds had calmly walked out of the kennels and gone wandering, so that when their feeding time came the enclosures were empty. Two of the hounds had sat on the railway line and stopped the evening train, and another had got on to a bus and chased everybody out and then gone to sleep on a seat. Another pair had hunted two kittens into the church porch and then played catch with them, leaving them unhurt but soaking wet with saliva. It had happened during the evening service. When the door was opened to see what was going on the two wet kittens had gone into the church, the hounds had looked in, sneezed very loudly, gone into the public bar of the Rose and Crown, behind the counter, and lapped up a great deal of beer and a tin of crisps. The huntsman had been out until midnight looking for them. Since the hounds had been in one pub he had to look in all, and in the end the two hounds last to be found had led him home.

Dr Wix went up to Swang during the day. He told David about it in the evening. Frank Watson had loaded the gatepost on to a cart, and pulled it half-way to the Jingle Stones, but on a slope it had tumbled off the cart, and lay immovable on a wet slope of grass, and he could do nothing more with it. The boggart had settled down rather. It had cracked two pot basins, and turned a bowl of milk that Mrs Watson had been going to skim. It had teased the pigs and made them squeal, and blocked the kitchen chimney with a bolus of small stones and clay, and the cat had left the house, and sat on the garden wall in the rain. But that, Frank Watson said, was the sort of behaviour expected of boggarts. They had put down milk and cakes for it, and it had eaten them, and swept the floor for them by morning, but not very well.

'Apparently it's just something you learn to live with,'

said Dr Wix. 'There's no cure, but they're going to call in the vicar if it gets too troublesome.'

'How can they be so calm?' said David. 'I should be worrying. I do worry, in fact.'

'Well, there's nothing like that in our family,' said Dr Wix. 'Nor in the house, I think. I'll put a stethoscope to it if there is, or put down a bowl of chloroform. It's bound to be susceptible to some of the ordinary reactions of this world, or it couldn't tweak the pigs or block the chimney. At the moment I don't know who my patient is at Swang: Mrs Watson or the boggart. If I cure one I cure the other. The trouble is, they both seem to be particularly healthy. Mrs Watson is hardly perturbed at all. It was only the fall that troubled her, and she has a few bruises. And so far as I can gather the boggart is in what they call rude health, for a boggart, at any rate.'

David was calm about it, but Keith thought something might visit him at any time. He had a good look out of his bedroom window before going to sleep. There was nothing but the lawn and the trimmed rose bushes and the wall beyond, and the low street farther down the hill, and the plain misty in the autumn. There was no sign of anything untoward.

5

THE police constable knew Keith's father perfectly well, but he still had to be official. He merely stood in the doorway and watched Keith eat his breakfast. His father was cleaning his shoes, ready to leave for the office. His brief-case was beside him. It had had its weekly cleaning the night before.

'How long have you been out?' said Keith's mother, in a tone that meant she would stand no nonsense, no matter how official the police visit was. It meant, too, that she was old enough to be the policeman's mother, if she had wanted to be; and since she hadn't actually been his mother at the moment he was born, she was going to be it now.

'Since about five, Mrs Heseltine,' said the constable.

'Sit down,' said Mrs Heseltine, 'and have a cup of tea. You look hot and flustered and impatient and clemmed.'

'I am gant,' said the constable. Then he thought he had so often met Mr Heseltine in court and in other ways, when they had sometimes agreed and sometimes not, that it would be both polite and comfortable to sit down for a moment.

'What did you want?' said Mr Heseltine. 'This time of day. I know it must be urgent, so don't you take any notice of my wife if you have to be going.'

'It's the pigs,' said the constable.

'Have they been tweaked?' said Keith.

'It depends what you mean by tweaked,' said the constable. 'The ones I'm talking about have been stolen. You know the piggery down at the bottom, by the station, Mr Heseltine?'

'I know more about it than most,' said Mr Heseltine. 'I had a lot to do with it when they had their planning appeal.' He was a solicitor, and that was how the constable knew him so well, through having to give evidence against his clients, and sometimes for them.

'Aye, well,' said the constable. 'There was a great piece of roof torn off in the night, and every pig was taken. I'm just going round to find out whether anyone this end of the town heard anything. Did you?'

'I didn't,' said Mr Heseltine. 'Not a squeak, or tweak.' Mrs Heseltine shook her head. 'There isn't much sound gets into this house,' she said. Keith said he had heard nothing. Not even, he thought but didn't say, a boggart.

'I'll be on my way,' said the constable. 'Just fancy,

more than two hundred pigs, fat as lard all of them, stolen just like that. There must have been no end of a noise, don't tell me.'

'There was a fair amount of noise when he began to put pigs in there,' said Mr Heseltine. 'There was a lot of complaint. If there had been as much as that when they were taken out, and all in one night, you'd have been able to hear it at the police station, never mind here.'

'Aggrieved parties, were there, Sir?' said the constable.

'There were,'' said Mr Heseltine. 'But I'm not sure I ought to tell you who they were. You can find out from plenty of other people, and I was professionally involved in it, so I ought not to say anything.'

'It's a line of investigation,' said the constable. 'I wonder how they got them away without a noise. You can't kill them without a squeal coming out, it's sort of held in the skin like the air in a balloon.'

When he had gone Keith finished his breakfast quickly, wanting to go up to David's and tell him what had happened.

'It couldn't be those hounds, could it?' said his mother, looking up from the paper.

'Not by themselves,' said Mr Heseltine. 'Clever thieves, that's all.'

David was still in his dressing-gown. He was delighted to hear about the pigs, and wanted to go down and have a look at once. He was made to have his breakfast first, though, and told not to be so pleased over other people's misfortunes.

'They'll be insured,' said Keith. 'They'd be worth about a thousand pounds, wouldn't they?'

'Two hundred of them?' said Dr Wix. 'I suppose so. Maybe more. I bet the party that owns them, and I know who it is but I'm naming no names, had more than two hundred in there, but isn't saying anything.'

'Why?' said Keith. 'He won't get them back if he doesn't.'

'He's only got a permit for two hundred,' said Dr Wix. 'I know that, and I suspect he's had more in than that. So he can't claim for any more than the permitted number, or he'll have his permission taken away.'

There was no way of getting near the robbed piggery. A police car was across the mouth of the lane leading to it, and there was a team of policemen working on the roof of the building, where there was a hole in the asbestos sheeting, and warmth still rising in the cold morning air.

At school most people had heard something about the matter; but it was not until boys from a little farther away began to come in that the story became strange. All the first comers were from the town, and their gossip was the piggery. The next comers were from the villages, and their story was the same. Their pigsties had been emptied in the night. The last arrivals had the same story, from remote farms and solitary places. All their pigs had been taken, boar, sow and sucklings. Fields and pig holes were bare of pigs. And no sound had been heard in the night.

'This'll drive the police frantic,' said David. 'It's all very well for Sherlock Holmes to say you can't have a theory until there isn't any need for one because the facts speak for themselves, and all that about taking away the impossible and leaving the probable and that's it. But you can't just vanish every pig in the district in complete silence, whether there's a theory or not.'

'It's like West Witton, over in Wensleydale,' said Keith, thinking of it and saying it at the same moment. 'They used to have trouble with a giant who stole their pigs until they got together and killed him. . . .' And then he realized what he had said. David realized it too,

94

and waited until he and Keith were alone before turning back to the remark.

'It just came into my head,' said Keith. 'Let's go up in the library and find out about it.'

'No need,' said David. 'I know it too, but giants and then pigs didn't come into my thick skull. Anyway, I was wrong. You don't need a theory to account for it. The facts do it well enough. It was a giant that took them, and we saw a giant. But I'm not going to the police with that tale.'

'A pig's tail,' said Keith. 'Nor me. We could be wrong, of course.'

'We're not wrong if it was a giant we saw,' said David. 'But I'm not going to admit a giant to anyone except you, even to myself. I wish you weren't a witness.'

At dinner-time, though, David could not bear the thought of so many policemen wasting their time searching for the human kind of clue. He and Keith went out of the school gates and rang up from a call box, using fourpence, instead of dialling the exchange and asking for the free police call.

When the police station came on the line David cleared his throat and said 'Why don't you look in the hills for the pigs? They're probably up there.'

There was a moment's hesitation at the other end, and a click on the line, and the officer who had answered said:

'Why don't you tell us a bit more about it? That would be more helpful. Where are you now, Sir?'

David covered the mouthpiece for a moment. 'I wish they didn't think I was joking,' he said. 'I can hear half a dozen of them on the line listening to me.'

'I don't know anything,' said David. 'It's just a reasonable guess.' Then he put the mouthpiece down.

'Fingerprints everywhere,' said Keith. 'And it's no

good wiping them off because they'll be even on the coins you put in the box.'

They left the box and went back to school. No one had any way of recognizing their fingerprints, and that was that.

No pigs were found that day, or the next day, or the day after. But the succeeding day was market day, and something happened on that day, though it seemed accidental that it was market day, and a pity too. On another day there would have been fewer people about.

There were police at the market, looking at incoming pigs from farther away, in case they could be identified. There were one or two suspect ones, but they were soon cleared and sold. Then the police left the market to look after itself, so far as pigs were concerned, and went back to their other business.

Keith and David saw some of the events of the market place, and Dr Wix saw the results, and the constable he knew had told him the rest, because he had been on the scene from the beginning. Dr Wix told the boys the background that evening.

'The police had been out on the moor most of the day,' he said. 'They had a hint from someone that the hills were the place to look.' David stared at the fire. 'And this morning they thought they saw a pig. You see, yesterday they came across any number of pig tracks. They thought the pigs must have been taken off a wagon up there, and loaded on to another, or something of the sort was tried, but the pigs got away. But they had to have something that was a clue, and the best clue would be one of the actual pigs from somewhere, and they would hope they could identify it, and get a lead that way. So they began to chase the pig they saw, and they got it cornered up above Swang, and into the lane. It came rushing down towards the town, so they rang up from Swang itself, to get it stopped before it ran into the road or into the river, and a couple of police went to the bottom of the lane that goes to Swang. They were the first two I saw. The creature got past them with no difficulty. And you know what happened next.'

David and Keith did know. The Market had been packing up when they came through the market place. The stalls were coming down, and the last bustle of the day was on. The buses were just about to be filled up, and many farmers and outlying villagers had stayed until this time to pick up children from school.

David and Keith were coming up the hill when the turmoil began. First there was the loud and continued blowing of a police whistle, shrilling above all the noise of the market place and the van and car engines. And then there was the movement of people getting away from something, and screams, and then shouts, some cheerful, because there often were cheerful shouts at four o'clock on market days, when the pubs closed. The cheerful shouts changed their tone. Something was going on in the busy part of the square, at the top. People were running away from it.

A stall fell down. It was the one that sold cloth. As it went down people scattered away from it, though one or two of the men poked at something with their sticks. From out of the wreckage something crawled. At first it was impossible to tell what it was, because a bolt of blue woollen cloth had unrolled on it. Then the thing underneath broke out, shaking its head angrily, and began to run along the cobbles, down the hill.

It was, in fact, the pig that the police had been chasing. But it was no ordinary pig. It was a great bristling grim grey wild boar, maddened by the market place, and going out of its way to side-swipe every moving thing it saw, in the hope of killing or discouraging it. It gashed

97

the tyre of a minicar that had started to move, and the minicar foundered. It ran towards people on the pavement, but down here people had more time to realize what had happened, and the shops filled suddenly with people who were buying nothing but safety. David and Keith stood still, with an eye on the bonnet of a car close by. The boar did not see them, and went down the square, to the corner, and round into the road to the station.

'Do something,' said David. 'We'll go down and shout to people to keep out of the way.'

But the police had had more time. There was the ringing of a bell, the roar of an engine, the flashing of lights, and a black police car came down the other side of the square, sounded its siren, and crossed along the bottom side and down into the same street as the boar. It gathered speed. There was a thud, and a shriek like a demon. The bell stopped, and the siren. There was the banging of a car door, and seven shots. And then quiet.

At the top of the square were four ambulances, and Dr Wix's car. Thirteen people had been gashed with tusks, nine more were hurt in the rush, and the two policemen at the end of the lane were taken to hospital too. There was blood on the cobbles. The dead boar was taken to the police station, and a zoologist called, because boars have not been wild in this country for two centuries.

6

' "DEPREDATIONS of wild pig",' David read, leaning over Keith's shoulder for marmalade.

'I wish you'd have your breakfast at home,' said Keith.

'You don't know how rare marmalade is in our house, because it only gets made once a year, and even then it isn't really believed in because the oranges aren't grown in the country.'

David had come down to Keith's house early with the local paper, earlier than Keith could have got it, because Dr Wix had been called down to the paper shop before five o'clock and brought his own morning editions back. He had come back to the house, roused David, and told him there was a job of paper delivery if he wanted it, because there was a special edition going to press at the paper shop that morning; not an edition of papers, but an edition of humans.

Keith finished his breakfast, and then he and David walked up to the paper shop. David had not had time to read more than the large print so far, but they could read the rest as they took the papers round. They paused outside the shop, and listened, to see whether the new edition was shouting its headlines. So far there was no news.

'Why it can't wait until tomorrow I don't know,' said Mr Fletcher, handing over bundles of papers. 'Tomorrow we don't work. It'll be a woman, depend on it, it's just like them.'

David read through the article he had started, a line at a time as they went up Finkle Street towards the estate. Before he did so he made the position clear to Keith.

'We shan't get a penny for this,' he said. 'It's all part of the National Health Service, Wix version. When Mr Fletcher sends the next paper bill it'll be marked "paid" already. So there's nothing for our pockets.'

'I wish it was snowing,' said Keith. 'I feel just like throwing a snowball at that wall.'

'Some people are not relevant,' said David. ' "Depredations of wild pig. A boar pig of the wild variety (*sus scrofa*) was discovered in the market place of Garebridge this week".'

'This is number seventeen,' said Keith. 'Let's be having that paper, David, if it's got seventeen on it.'

For the rest of the paper round David read snatches of the paper between houses, and then delivered it into the box. There was not a great deal of new knowledge in the paper. They had seen the pig themselves, and observed more than the reporter. They found out its Latin name, and that *sus scrofa* was the European wild boar, and that on a post-mortem examination the beast's stomach had been full of acorns and heather shoots, that it appeared to be five years old, and had an old wound, possibly a spear wound on its shoulder. And that was all. No one had any idea where it had come from. No zoo, public or private, no landowner, no one, would admit to having lost a specimen of wild boar.

Another column was about pigs too: the domesticated pigs that had been stolen from the piggery and from the surrounding farms. The farms that had lost pigs were all in Vendale. No one further afield had reported any loss. No one had seen any trace of them. A little note by the editor himself on the middle page said that there was no known connexion between the wild boar and the domesticated ones.

'But that,' said David, folding the paper he was reading and putting it through a letter box, 'is unlikely. There must be a connexion. Obviously pigs mean giants and giants mean wild boars. So there is a link.'

'You're not being logical again,' said Keith. 'But I agree with you. At least, I would if it wasn't for one thing. I don't think we saw a giant, really. It must have been an effect of vision, or the sunlight, or a cloud going up the hill.'

'You've got to have a sort of belief,' said David. 'I'll

have to show you more evidence. I'll show you some I haven't seen myself, when we've finished the round.'

After that they read no more papers. They were left at the bottom of the town with two empty sacks and a feeling that it was a long time since breakfast and a long time before school.

'Wix's good deed done for the day,' said David. 'Let's go down to the piggery.'

'I'm going to make you find the evidence,' said Keith. 'I won't let you wriggle out of it.'

'You might have to,' said David. 'It's only an inspiration, and it doesn't explain wild boars.'

He found his evidence. The piggery was still being watched over by the police; or by one of them at any rate. When he saw people approaching, he stopped being a man in navy blue leaning against a building and became a stiff policeman again. He walked to the wall beside the land to the piggery. David and Keith were in the field alongside.

'Now,' he said, 'have you any business here?'

'No,' said David. 'Just looking for clues. We don't need to come in.'

It was the policeman who had visited the Heseltines the morning before, so he was not coldly unfriendly. He said he couldn't let them in, on any account; but he was quite glad to see someone. He wouldn't have minded seeing a villain, he said; but he had merely been on watch here from midnight on, and only seen his colleagues at intervals. It was just his luck to watch all night and not see a villain of any sort.

'It isn't every sort you want to see,' said David. 'But we'll go past and look for clues over there.'

David looked at the morning grass, dewy by the time of day and faded brown by the time of year. He was trying to make the low morning light tell him something.

'This is it,' he said, when he had cast around for a time. 'Stand here, Keith, and you'll see it too.' He pointed out what Keith had to look for: going across the field there was a double line of indentations. As if a giant had walked from the river to the piggery, and back again.

'I don't like the idea,' said Keith. But David made him follow to the edge of the river. There, in the sandy bank, there was the sort of indentation feet make from a standing jump. David made a standing jump close by, to show that the holes he made were the same shape. The only difference was in size. The marks they had found were eight times bigger than the ones David made.

On the opposite bank was the landing place.

'He put one foot in the water,' said Keith. 'I've done it myself before now.'

'Then you believe too,' said David. 'Who else could jump across the river?'

'You've proved it,' said Keith. 'Shall we go and tell the policeman?'

'I can imagine the scene,' said David. 'No. We'll go across the river and see where he went from there.'

To cross the river they, as human beings, had to go back to the road, cross the bridge, and then go into the fields again, and round the outside of the bend in the river. They came on the trail easily enough, where the giant had walked down the fields and up them again, and then gone into the thickety wood that hung there on the side of the hill. In the thickety wood the evidence was stronger, because the passage of the giant had knocked the undergrowth about a great deal, laying it flat and cracking the spindly growth, and even pushing aside quite well-grown trees, so that earth and stones started from the roots, and the roots themselves followed, and the trees leaned.

There was a curved path through the wood. If it had

been a straight way through no doubt someone would have seen it and looked already.

There were traces of pig: footprints and dung, and on some of the trees white hair and mud, where a wet pig that had swum the river had had a luxurious scratch.

'You can't quite hear them,' said Keith.

The route led out beyond the hill-top, through a gateway and over two more fields. There was a first set of giant prints, overlaid by the returning pigs, and overlaying the pig prints the second, returning giant prints. Now they just showed if the ground was the slightest bit soft, when they would break the skin of the turf.

'He must weigh in tons,' said David. 'Just keep an eye open, will you.'

'We shall have to go back any minute now,' said Keith. 'Or we'll be late for assembly.'

'We'll just get to the moor edge,' said David. 'Then we'll run back and be slightly sweaty all day.'

'I'm slightly sweaty all day already,' said Keith. 'Tugging up this bank. It takes a bit of doing.'

'There's two of us,' said David. 'I wouldn't have come alone, would you?'

'It depends who runs fastest when we do see him,' said Keith. 'The one at West Witton wasn't all that friendly, was he?'

The natural road to follow was the one that led to the moor gate. The gateway was still there, but the gate itself had been broken down, as if a great foot had been put through it, and then another. The giant did not know how to open gates; any more than he had known how to open the doors of the piggery: he must have ripped off the roof and taken the pigs out through the gap. Keith looked back on what he knew, and thought that a logical mind would have concluded that giants were involved, from the piece of evidence alone. But policemen, he supposed, had to confine their deductions to things already known about and existing. Giants are not facts.

Inside the moor the trail was harder to follow. Keith found a promising one, of pig tracks, going along a little sheep trod, and David found another. They went in different directions, which was no help if the pigs were wandering at random.

'The thing to do is take a wide cast round,' said David. 'If they did stay together to cross the moor there'll be a bunch of tracks somewhere, and that's what we want to find. But we ought to go back.'

'We'll just go up on the first crest of the hill,' said Keith. 'We might find the lot, mightn't we?'

'One thing leads to another,' said David. 'We'll be coming to the Jingle Stones before we know where we are. Just one ridge, then, and that's all.'

They climbed the first ridge. In the little valley beyond there was a black lump. Keith thought it was a shooting butt, made from peaty turf. But David sniffed and said he could smell fire. Keith looked at the black lump. It was peat; but as well as peat there was wood in the pile, and coming from it, hardly showing against the further hill, but steamy against the clear sky with its elevated clouds, there was smoke.

They went down to the fire with caution. But as they came nearer they saw that it lay in a cleared patch, where the ling was not growing and perhaps never had; and round it there was nothing to be seen; or at any rate nothing so large as a giant.

David stopped and looked at Keith. 'It has a very gone-away feeling,' he said. 'Gone away just now, I mean, like the table laid in the *Mary Celeste*. Back-any-minute-like.'

'We'd see him coming,' said Keith, looking round in case he did. He thought he saw a flutter on the horizon behind him, but it did not come again, and he thought it must be a bird that had flown off out of sight the other way.

Then they came on the bones, close against the fire, and more than bones, the smell of roast pork.

'This is it,' said David. 'We've actually followed the tracks a lot better than the police.'

'Is it pig?' said Keith. 'It's just like ribs,' and he ran his hand over his own bones, finding that they were sculptured in much the same way.

'Pig's head-bone,' said David, turning over a darkened mass that was against the grey ash of burnt wood. 'It's disgusting and cannibalistic and a bit sick-making, but it's only a roast pig that someone's eaten.'

'It's like the inside of a dustbin,' said Keith. 'It hadn't any table manners, whatever cooked and ate this.'

'Let's go,' said David; because the plain thought that something not human had killed, cooked and eaten a pig up here, was too immediate and large. It was a thought that should be come to gradually, and not thrust straight into the mind on the site of the event; particularly when the fallen charred bones were still warm and the crackling smelt rather pleasant.

Then there was a thump behind them, and an arm went round each of their waists and held tight.

Part Three

ON HARE TROD

'Oh, come now,' said Dr Tate. 'Arrested I can understand, but released again, that I can't believe.'

'They looked at us, Sir,' said David. 'And then they decided we couldn't possibly have the learning to commit a crime. Then they let us go.'

Dr Tate had been in a quaint humour ever since David and Keith had arrived at school that day. Of course, they had come in very late, just at the end of morning break; and there was no hope of avoiding that bright eye under the silver hair: Dr Tate saw everything and often heard everything too. Now he sat behind his desk, one set of his attention on David and Keith, and the other set on the yard outside.

'We shall get nowhere by slanging each other, Wix,' he said. It was not that his quaint humour changed to something quainter. Dr Tate had no sudden edge over which he was pushed by anything. His mood was fixed and decided before he adopted it. David was always trying to rationalize it and find an explanation for the very diverse faces Dr Tate showed from day to day. Today's face he had met fleetingly now and then, when something glittered in the discourse of the schoolroom, as if a leaf had unwrapped itself just under the surface of the ground and moved the dust.

Keith, though, thought that Dr Tate was a kind but tedious man. Dr Tate knew what Keith thought.

'You teased first, Sir,' said David.

'That's true,' said Dr Tate. 'The sergeant telephoned from the police station and told me you were there. He said you would be able to tell me why without any embarrassment. But I never ask questions. I only make comment. But I see you are embarrassed. Well, you may convince the police, but I don't think you have any hope of convincing – yourselves.'

'It's the pig business,' said David. 'Keith and I found out where the pigs went after they were taken from the piggery. We followed the track up the hill. Then we found a fire and a roasted pig. It had been finished, though.' Then David stopped, because the next thing was embarrassing. As they had stood by the soggy peat fire, with its steamy reek round their heads, wondering who had slaughtered and eaten, something had encircled each of their waists and held them.

David remembered the moment, two hours ago, when he thought a giant had taken them. Keith remembered it too, and he remembered the sky blackening overhead and the whole focus of the landscape changing, and a sound that had begun cutting itself off. Then he had been on the heather with cold fingers at his throat. And there would always be with him the thought that giants have cold fingers.

But it was not a giant. It was a police constable, comforting him in his swoon. And the sergeant had been talking to David, and looking at the remains of the pig.

It had all been very suspicious, the sergeant said, the way they had said they would find out what had happened, and then gone across the river and up the far bank in the trees. The constable had told him, and between them they had made out a smashed track up the woodland, and followed. And now would they give the best account they could of why they had gone the way they had gone, and found what they had found?

It was no good mentioning giants. Keith's faint had to be left as a symptom of guilt, though not a serious one. All that was left was a suspicion in the sergeant's mind that he had not been told everything; that perhaps the two boys had seen the pigs being taken, or knew from other sources how and why it had been done. They had drunk tea at the police station, and not even been asked to make a statement. And now they were at school.

'I see,' said Dr Tate, when he had heard what he called the bones of the story. 'I'm afraid you aren't going to like this, either of you. But there are certain reasons why it would have been better for you to stay away until after dinner today. You'll find out why.'

Then they had gone back into school. The dinner was roast pork. Keith felt very delicate about it, but David was all right until he found a piece of bone. Then he had to leave the rest. He had touched bone in the peaty ground and turned the pig's head.

At the police station the sergeant had explained why an arm had gone round each waist. It was to keep them both still, so that they did not trample the ground any more and destroy clues; and it had been partly a good joke, following a piece of silent tracking. The sergeant had not, of course, known that giants were in anyone's mind. Nor had he ever suspected them of doing any more than they had said: detecting.

In the quiet evening time Keith went up to David's house and let himself in at the door. There was a faint whiff of ether from the surgery. David was by the fire tracing the transverse sentences of a Horation ode down the page and finding ellipsis and caesura, dactyl and spondee. Anything, he said, but the meaning. 'These things are like old man Tate. It's not so much what he says, but what track he's running on at the time. He's got a multitrack mind, and you can't tell which station he's aiming for. I think this Horace wrote in a way we don't have nowadays, about places that don't exist any more, in a language that isn't used. But I don't mind. It's rather nice to find things you can recognize like apple orchards damp with wandering streams. Or Lydia telephoning somebody.' But that was a joke.

David put the books away, because now there was a whole week-end ahead, and there was no need to work on Friday night.

'We'll go into my room,' he said. 'And experiment with that candle. I'll go and get it.'

A moment later he brought the little flame into the house, sheltering it needlessly against the wind. The wind did not disturb it. With it he brought an inverted test tube.

'This I've had over it,' he said, 'to catch the products of combustion. We'll see whether it's carbon dioxide. Or at least, we'll see whether it's oxygen.'

'It won't be anything,' said Keith. 'It isn't burning. I mean, it doesn't burn away, so it can't produce anything. And what's more, if it doesn't produce heat, but only cold, then the gases it does make, if it makes any, won't go up into the tube at all.'

'Be scientific,' said David. 'Find out by experiment.'

They found nothing out. A glowing splinter went out in the test tube, but it meant nothing, because a glowing splinter went out in another test tube that was filled with the best of outdoor air, at the window.

'So we don't know anything,' said David. He opened a drawer and brought out a thick lens, and looked at the flame with it. They had an ordinary candle as a comparison. It had a lusty yellow flame that bent and smoked in every movement of air, that dribbled wax, that was hot, and smelt, that curled its wick over and left blackness in its own cup of melted wax, and was, beside the other, a hobbledehoy sort of creature with no manners. David studied their flames in turn. He said 'Hmn' in a wise voice, but was silent when Keith asked him to back up the statement with something more definite. He put the lens in front of the household candle and projected its image on to the wall, where it flickered and danced upside down. The candle that Nellie Jack John had left would not project itself on to the wall at all, though they blew out the competition.

David studied the flame with his naked eye. 'It's like looking into the fire,' he said. 'I think I can begin to see things.'

He looked up when he spoke. Keith was standing at his left side; but David looked to his right, and spoke to the empty air, looking up as if he were looking into a face.

'I'm here,' said Keith, and David turned his head sharply.

'Dazzled,' he said. 'I thought it was you but it was the wardrobe or the curtain or something. You know how you can get by one sort of fence in the twilight and your eyes cross themselves and you can't tell how far away the fence is? Well, I did that then.'

He went back to looking at the flames. He said there was movement in it, and some shapes, which he was sure were significant, but they changed too much. He went on looking, to see whether he could capture them.

Keith felt uneasy about it. He was sure that David was paying too much attention to the flame, that it was attracting him too much. He wondered if he was being selfish and in a way jealous; but it was not that. It was a sense of discomfort, of danger, almost, that had come to him. He felt that there was an indulgent wickedness in looking into the flame.

He put his hand down, between David's face and the candle. David looked up, then stood up.

'You're right,' he said. Then he began to walk across the room, with his hands in the air in front of his face.

'Dazzled,' he said. But he did not walk quite as if he were dazzled. He walked as if something real were round him, something that had to be pushed aside sometimes, or avoided. Then he sat on the bed, and seemed to be waiting.

'It sank into my eyes,' he said. 'I was full of it.'

'Let's take it outside again,' said Keith. 'That would be best.'

'It'll be all right up here,' said David, quite firmly, so that Keith knew the candle would stay here in the room. 'Put it in the tin on the mantelpiece.'

Keith took it up and dropped it into the tin, and put the lid down on it. Then they went down to the red fire, and sat beside it, saying nothing to each other. David was thinking of other things, but Keith did not know that. At last he let himself out, though David came to the door with him and watched him go. Keith went home, still oppressed by the thought of the candle, up there in David's room like a creature from another place and time.

He looked back at the house. The light went on in David's room, and then went out. But there was still a tiny glimmer from between the curtains, and a white light showing.

There was something wrong. But Keith went home, in spite of the feeling that he should go back and stay with David longer.

The uneasiness stayed with him all night, and until he came to David's house in the middle of the morning.

David was no longer dazzled and strange. Keith wiped out all the thoughts that had come to mind in the darkness, thoughts of unformed danger, thoughts of the incomprehensible darkness beyond the solitary gleam of the candle. Yesterday's strangeness, he thought, was due to the morning's experience, which had left him edgy, and left David tired. There was no more to it than that. But he did inquire about the flame.

'I looked at it a bit longer,' said David. 'But I didn't find anything out about it. I can see things in it, but they aren't real things, are they?'

'Of course not,' said Keith. 'You were hypnotizing yourself, that's all. You could have done it with anything.'

'That's what I thought in the end,' said David. 'You can get a sort of dizziness looking at the face of an alarm clock in the middle of the night when you don't know which way up your head is and you can't tell the time properly. The specks of light eat into you. It's to do with the cells of the brain, that's all, and the cells of the eye.'

'That's it,' said Keith. 'What shall we do?'

They read the morning's paper. It had been delivered by Mr Fletcher today, now that he was the father of a boy (DOUGLAS KEVIN, a brother for ALISON) and now that it was written in the first column of the paper. The weekly bill, that came with the papers, was not marked paid. All that was crossed off was the delivery charge, which was twopence.

'Penny a name,' said Keith. 'Do you think there's something a bit mean about Mr Fletcher?'

'An economical spirit showing itself,' said David. 'I wonder what else his paper says. You and I are no worse off, anyway, because we weren't expecting anything.'

The rest of the paper was more surprising. Among the reports of Rural District Councils, accounts of whist drives, lists of mourners, headlines of THIRSK MAN DROVE DANGEROUSLY and RIPON OPPOSES BOUNDARY CHANGES and YOUNG RIDERS SUCCESSFUL AT THORNTON-LE-DALE, there was half a column on the Jingle Stones. It was a follow-up of last week's report on the disturbance near them. The reporter had been up again:

'. . . up the steep path to this historic monument possibly older than Stonehenge, only to find that the stone circle was *Continued in next column*.'

But in the next column there was no sign of the end of the article, nor anywhere on the page. A close scrutiny of the whole paper did not bring the missing lines to light. They had been lost.

'We'll go up again,' said David. 'We'll find out about them, and then we'll write that letter to the editor.'

2

THE letter to the editor was never to be written. David thought out a few general purpose phrases which could be used no matter what the letter meant, and noted them down on a piece of paper. Then Keith left him and went home for his dinner, and to do a little prep before coming out again. It was the week-end, the time among days that once seemed to him eternal, and now seemed minutely finite, a mouse of time threatening the enormous cat of work to be done. Often the cat merely sat on the mouse and nothing got done. Sometimes, by some subtle skill and not mere strength, the mouse overcame.

When Keith came back to David's house at two o'clock, Dr Wix was just going out for a short afternoon round. 'David's upstairs,' he said.

Keith went up and into David's room. David was sitting in darkness, with the curtains drawn across the window. Yet it was not quite darkness, because on the table in front of him was the candle, like a pygmy spirit erect over the wood, reflected in the mahogany like the ghost of a ghost.

David was looking into the flame, not moving, not apparently awake even, except that his eyes were open. His hands were under his chin and his knuckles were clenched white. Keith saw it in the light that came through the door with him.

'David,' he said. David did not respond. Keith left the door open, and pulled the curtains back. David still sat there as if he were cast in wax himself. Keith did not pause to let thoughts about anything creep into his mind. He touched David on the shoulder, and David woke up.

'Hello,' he said, looking round the room as if he could not see anything.

'You've dazzled yourself,' said Keith, in an impatient scolding tone, the one used for talking to people who have done something they have the real sense not to do.

'Yes, that's it,' said David. Then he began to look for Keith in a slightly different way, as if something had come between them, something visible only to David.

'I'm going to throw that candle away again,' said Keith.

'No, I will,' said David, turning and seeing the flame clearly enough. There was no shadow between him and it. He picked the candle up, and dropped it into the tin it had been living in.

'We'll dump it outside somewhere,' he said.

'I don't know why you look into it,' said Keith. But he thought he did know. He could imagine that there must be some fascination of vision in the flame, something that held the eyes, something that perhaps ought not to be looked at, something that David knew should not be gazed at; because there he was, standing by the table and blinking slightly, and looking a little ashamed.

'Come on,' said Keith, feeling suddenly that he was in charge of David and his thoughts, instead of David being in charge of him.

David was himself again by the time they reached the back door. But there was still something behind his ordinary self, and he did not want to get rid of the candle.

'I tell you what,' said Keith. 'You're addicted to it.'

'I know,' said David. 'I want to go on looking. It shows me things.'

'What things?' said Keith. 'Be scientific.'

'There's things moving,' said David. 'Things inside the flame. And it's not just the rods and cones in my eyes. They're there, you know, but they aren't like sight at all. It's like looking out into time or space or infinity. It's like seeing everything at once. It's like getting out of a train that's going along and seeing it go along, and being independent and part of it at the same time. It's like looking at everywhere at once from everywhere at once.'

'It'll be bad for you,' said Keith. 'You'll be better off without it. You know where that candle came from. Nellie Jack John brought it out, and we don't know where he'd been, do we?'

'I looked at it nearly all night,' said David. 'And now I'm not looking at it, but I can still see things. But don't worry, I know which are real.'

'I don't like you being like that,' said Keith. 'Drop it in the dustbin or something.'

David put the candle in its tin in the shed where it had lived already for several weeks. As soon as he put it down he said his head was clearer, and there was more day than he remembered. But almost at once he stepped off the pavement to walk round something that was not there. When Keith asked him he would not say what he thought he had seen.

They went out on to Hare Trod, and up towards the Jingle Stones, which was where they expected to find material for a letter to the editor.

Hare Trod was deserted. It went first through fields. In one there were bullocks, and in another sheep, and a tup with a rudded belly. Higher up there was the moorland beginning, and down to one side the farm called Swang, with smoke at the chimney.

'I wonder about that boggart,' said David. 'Do you think we should call?'

'Perhaps you'll be able to see it,' said Keith, in not quite the kindest tone he could have employed.

'I was only dazzled,' said David. 'I can see perfectly well now.'

They went higher, ridge after ridge peaking the Trod under their feet. Keith looked out over the valley to the far side. He saw people walking on the far hill. He was going to point them out to David and show him how small they were in comparison with the giant they had seen a week ago, when he realized that at the distance they were away he could never have picked out people with such clarity. He was seeing giants again, and not one only, but six or seven.

David saw them too. They stood on the Trod and watched. The giants were playing. They had something that looked like a ball, and they were throwing it about.

'It's a game,' said David. 'There are two sides, and a goal at each end of the pitch.'

'They don't take any notice of the walls,' said Keith. 'It's as if they were a foot high only. And the goal is that barn at the top of the fields. Look, they keep throwing the ball towards it, and one of them defends it.'

'It's not a ball,' said David. 'It's a rock, and if they hit that barn with it they'll cave it in.'

Then a goal was scored, and the front of the barn was caved in, and the firm outline of the roof ridge sagged.

That finished the game. The ball, or rock, was cast down towards the bottom of the valley, and the players left the pitch and went striding up the hill and over the crest and out of sight. They had been called by another, larger giant, who strode up behind them, looked at the damaged barn, pulled something out of it, and walked off with the thing tucked under his arm.

Keith looked at David. 'It was a cow,' he said. 'He took a cow. He carried it off with him, under his arm.'

'They must have finished the pigs,' said David; and it would have been an amusing remark if it hadn't been about giants.

'Just a quick look at the Jingle Stones, and then back home,' said Keith. 'We can't tell anyone though, can we?'

'I'm not going to be the first to mention it,' said David. 'That's all.'

The Trod twisted itself, and then went on. They walked round the twisted part of the path. Then David stopped.

'It's funny,' he said. 'The Trod doesn't do that, except at the Jingle Stones.'

He was right. The path made a little detour to go round the Jingle Stones. And this was the place where the detour should be. But the Jingle Stones were not there. In the places where they had stood were little pits, like the healed-over sockets when teeth have been drawn, except that these sockets had not healed over with grass. The sand that they had seen before had run down and smoothed the edges of the holes. But the stones that had stood here were gone, and there was no trace of them.

They went up the Trod, to the edge of the peat moss, where the moor stretched level for a mile or more. They had looked in the right place. The Jingle Stones had never stood higher up. They had looked in the right place...

David came down to the site, and sat on the edge of a hole, looking at the ground.

'I'm thinking,' he said. 'I'm thinking what I would

have done if I was a Jingle Stone. It's not logic in the ordinary way.'

'You don't say,' said Keith. 'Let's get back home.'

'Wait on,' said David. 'I can see with the eyes of a stone, and think with its thoughts, and feel with its layers and strata, and I just stand whilst the world rushes by like a wind. I think the wind is time. And then time stops and I can get out of where I'm standing, and I'm a person again.'

Keith thumped David severely on the shoulder. David stood up. 'It's an understanding I've got,' he said. 'I understand it from looking into the flame. I know what it is. I know.'

'Shut up,' said Keith, feeling uneasy, as if something were behind him: not behind his body so much as behind his eyes, where it would never be seen. 'Shut up and come home. I don't like it when you're acting like this.'

'No need to be frightened of me,' said David. 'I'm only talking about things that exist. They're only almost strange, not absolutely strange.'

Keith pulled him to his feet and set him to walk down the Trod again. 'We'll go to Swang,' he said. 'And see Frank Watson. And the boggart.'

'I shan't be able to see that,' said David.

But the boggart could see him. They left the Trod and walked down the little valley to Swang, and into the lane and through the gate. Frank Watson was foddering, but not too busy to be able to talk.

'Now then, David,' he said. 'You'll have heard of our visitor from your father?'

'We just came by to ask about it,' said David. 'We went up to look at the Jingle Stones.'

'They've gone missing,' said Frank Watson. 'Well, they say there's never one strange thing, don't they? Not that our boggart's all that strange, you see. It's been in the family, or the house, or both, for a long time. Mebbe it knows about the Jingle Stones. I don't know that you'll hear it. We've fed it up and fed it up, and it must be that fat it's content. It was always like that, times it would be about, and times it would be asleep, hibernating like. But I tell you,' and here he began to talk low, 'we never got much use out of it. Them fellows is supposed to do a bit about the house, sweeping up and cleaning the pots, but he's gitten a right lazy rascal and doesn't do a hand's turn, bar upsetting the pots or rolling up the rugs or working the springs out of the chair, or taking the plugs out of the tractor, and generally cussing on and banging. Go in to Mrs Watson, and see.'

Before they had got into the house Keith felt his ankle nipped. He thought it would be a creeping silent dog, but the dog was tied up by the pig hole. Keith wriggled his foot, and something rushed across the hay-strewn yard, and the front door of the farm swung open, and closed with a bang. Mrs Watson appeared in the doorway. Over her head appeared the teapot, swinging through the air. David thought it would fall to the ground, but it didn't. It landed at his feet, and the lid rattled.

Mrs Watson laughed. 'It's him,' she said. 'The good little fellow.'

'Did he bring it to me?' said David. 'Shall I say thank you?'

'You try that,' said Mrs Watson. David said it, then picked the pot up, and followed Mrs Watson into the house. He found a chair nudging him behind the knees, and he sat down. Then he thought a cat had jumped into his lap, but there was nothing there when he looked.

'Performance over, I hope,' said Mrs Watson.

'No,' said David. 'I didn't sit down on my own. I was put here. And there's something on my lap now.'

'Quick, then,' said Mrs Watson, 'hand down this saucer of milk.'

David took the saucer, and held it at knee level. There
was movement, but no weight, at his knee, and the saucer
emptied. Then, when every drop had gone, the saucer
left his hand and cracked against Keith's head, and fell
to the ground. Then David's lap was empty, and the
farm cat was hurrying round the table looking over its
shoulder.

'That's how it is,' said Mrs Watson. 'That's how it is
all the time. But there, I married into the family, I'll have
to put up with it. It was worse with Frank's mother. She
was more of a trial. This one doesn't speak. There's
worse things than that you can have in a house.'

'He likes me,' said David. 'Do you think it'll follow
me home?'

'Oh,' said Mrs Watson, 'I wouldn't like to see it go, no
I wouldn't.'

3

'How did you get on with him?' said Frank Watson,
when Keith and David were outside again. He had finished moving hay, and was up in the doorway of the
barn, the upper floor, standing at the top of the outside
stair.

'Not so bad,' said David. 'He liked me.'

'You're welcome,' said Frank Watson. 'He's a rotten
little . . .' But they did not hear the word that followed,
because there was a disturbance in the hay behind Frank,
and something began scooping it up and dredging it out
over his head, so that he was out of sight under a fall of
hay. The fall spread on to the steps, and became an ava-
lanche and a whirlwind all in one. Then it stopped and

Frank Watson stood up. He had been forced down the steps by the weight of moving hay. He pulled strands from his hair and from his eyes, and ran his finger round inside his neck where the hayseeds had stuck.

'I'll put it back,' he said, without any emotion in his voice at all. 'I shouldn't help if I were you. It would be better if I put it back myself.'

David wanted to help, though; and Frank thought they might risk it. He indicated the fact by handing a fork to David and putting on a sort of innocent look, because he dared not speak.

The boggart did not mind the hay being put back by David. David had guessed he was favoured in some way, or perhaps even feared a little. When he and Frank had almost finished David stopped, stood on the top step, and said, 'Come here, boggart.'

There was a rustling in the hay at his feet, but there was nothing to be seen. Frank Watson walked down the steps quickly, and stood to one side, in case there was more trouble.

'Now, boggart,' said David, 'put the rest back like a good fellow, and then.'

There was a sweeping noise, and hay gathered itself into a little mound, like the jockeys made on damp days in the field. The jockey rolled itself up the last two steps, growing bigger as it went, and rolled into the barn.

'Thank you,' said David. There was a thump in the barn, and the door closed, and the bolt went across. Then the boggart raced across the yard, knocking off Frank's hat, and tying a series of hard little knots in Keith's hair, so that his scalp was pulled up uncomfortably. The door of the farm opened, and there was quiet outside.

'Well, that's it then,' said Frank Watson. 'I wouldn't do that, I can tell you.'

'I'm beginning to know about things like that,' said

David. 'But I don't know everything. I don't know what's happened to the Jingle Stones.'

'You wouldn't be far wrong if you guessed the nearest thing, I dare say,' said Frank. 'Not so far out at that.'

'It isn't his sort of thing,' said David. 'He isn't very big. About the size of the cat.'

'Them little uns is good uns,' said Frank. 'But I'll be off now and move some sheep. Are you going up or downbank?'

'Upbank,' said David. 'We'll go back down the Trod.'

'Wait on,' said Frank. 'I'll go part way with you.' He went into his meal house and brought out a bucket with a few calf nuts in, and walked with the boys up a couple of fields. He left them there, and waited for his sheep to come to him, or to the bucket of nuts.

Keith and David went back towards the Trod. The sheep Frank was looking for were at the far end of his field, but he did not want to walk so far. He rattled the bucket. The sheep looked up, and made up their minds slowly, taking another bite whilst they did so.

'What a lot of them,' said David. 'Where have they come from?'

'There's fifteen,' said Keith. 'That's all.'

'No,' said David, 'far more, dozens and dozens, all moving round and round in circles.'

'No,' said Keith. 'They're all standing stupidly about. But they'll run down to Frank Watson in a moment.'

'I'm seeing things, then,' said David. 'I thought I might be. I can't get that dazzle out of my eyes. I wonder if I've hurt them.'

'Perhaps that candle gives off coherent light, like a laser,' said Keith. 'Because there's only a few sheep there.'

There was something more than the sheep. As Keith spoke the sheep moved, but not in the way he had

125

expected. They began to mill about, going in all directions, but always coming back towards the centre of the group they were making. They began to run, rather than walk and to call in a pitiful way; but sheep naturally and always call in a pitiful way.

'What do you see?' said Keith.

'It's like a big millwheel on the field,' said David. 'Lying flat, but very big, and quite clear and real. What do you see?'

'Fifteen sheep in a stampede,' said Keith.

Frank Watson had seen what was happening, and he came running over the grass. Then he too was caught up in the mill, and then, with the sheep, was thrown down, and the bucket rattled on the grass. A few seconds later the sheep were all calm, and were nosing in the grass for the nuts. And across the field came the shallow indentation in the grass that they had first seen in High Keld when the hounds were chased away. The grass moved under the thing.

'Can you see it?' said David.

'I can see where it is,' said Keith. 'What is it like?'

'Like a beehive,' said David. 'Can you hear it?'

But Keith could hear nothing. The thing like a beehive, but invisible, furrowed its way along the edge of the wall, and went down the hill.

'Come on,' said David. 'Let's see what else there is. There's only your fifteen sheep in the field now, so it isn't my eyes. Do you think I'm getting a power over things? If you looked in the candle flame I'm sure you'd get the power too.'

'Like heck,' said Keith.

When they came on to Hare Trod again Frank Watson was at the top of his field, looking round, with the sheep nudging the bucket that had held the nuts.

'Anything about?' said Keith.

'No,' said David. 'But I don't like it here now. The air seems to be full of something. I think we should go home. I don't like it here at all. Can you feel something tingling at you?'

Keith was busy, as he had been since they left Swang, taking tangles out of his hair. 'It's a bit close,' he said. 'If the sky was a bit cloudier it would mean thunder.'

'I'm sweating with it,' said David. 'But it isn't the weather. There's something else. There's something up here, but I can't quite get through to it.'

'Let's get through to our teas,' said Keith. 'I don't like you like this, and I think you're a fool for looking at that candle, and I think it gives off fumes or something, and one way and another it's got at you.'

They walked down the Trod after that in silence. Once David almost spoke, and then closed his mouth. Keith had been uneasy at first, because he did not like David to speak strangely, and he was not sure that talking about the candle was to the point. Now David began to look pale and worried, and no longer swung his arms, but held them to his side.

Then, at the next ridge, where another horizon opened below them, David stood still.

'Listen,' he said, 'listen, that's it.'

Keith could hear nothing. There was not even any wind to mark his hearing. The ground itself was dry and silent. When it is wet it always speaks. No sound came up from the town, which was out of sight, and no beasts spoke in nearby fields.

'This is it,' said David, and he stretched out his arms, first ahead of him, and then above his head. 'This is all I've ever wanted. Look at the butterfly, look.'

A sense of dread came on Keith, helpless dread and fear. His knees trembled and his heart quaked. On the desolate, sightless moor, beyond every house, on the narrow path to nowhere, a vision was visiting David, a lone vision that he could not share. And all that Keith knew about it was that it should not be so. It was not that David was doing wrong, or that wrong was being done to him, but that what was happening should not happen.

Then the thing did happen. David reached up towards something, something that Keith could not see, the butterfly he had spoken of. And all that Keith could see was a line black across the sky, black across the skyline, black across the fields, not on them like a pigment, but in them, like a dark crack no wider than a hair. It was a clear darkness, with the clearness (and Keith felt foolish as he thought it) of bramble jelly, and with the same paling towards the edge, so that the dark grew out of the light.

The crack swung towards them, and then gathered David up in itself. Keith saw him go, taken up into something that did not open up to receive him, but absorbed him. Then the crack in earth and sea and sky vanished too, and Keith felt himself rolling over and over on the grass, the green of it and the lightness of the whole sky alternating in front of his eyes.

He lay on his face, able to breathe in but unable to breathe out, with his limbs moving on their own and causing him pain where his hands beat the turf and his knees scraped themselves on a stone. There was a stunning silence round his head as if he had gone deaf. Then the grass, no more than six inches from his face, came rushing up to meet him, appearing to come at a tremendous pace, and yet to take all time to reach him. And then there was blackness.

Somebody moved him. He could feel his limbs being moved by other hands now, and his head was turned. He heard the voices of sheep, and the rattle of a bucket, and there was a hand on his heart. He could not move.

He did not want to move at the moment, and he had forgotten how to. He had almost forgotten that he could. Moving did not seem necessary. Nor did looking. Only breathing went on, as if someone else were doing it.

Then he seemed to be walking in spite of himself, though his feet were not feeling the ground at all, and there was still darkness. He felt himself going in and out of life, swinging from nowhere back into a place he began to know more and more, and to recognize: the world.

His eyes opened. He found he was not walking, but hung upside down over someone's back, looking at a rough tweed coat that smelt of sheep dung and stale milk. He was being carried on Frank Watson's back, down the hillside, with the grass moving away blurred at Frank's heels.

His body came alive. He stiffened. Frank's shoulder tipped forward, and he was set down on the grass. He was not able to sit up. He lay there propped up on one elbow, with Frank holding the other, and his head rolled about on his neck, and weakness would not be overcome.

'Away, then,' said Frank, and lifted him again, and carried him a long way, across grass, and then across the yard of the farm, and into the porch, and through the door. Keith heard voices, but did not understand what they were saying. There was the rattle of quick feet on wood, and then he was being taken upstairs, and was laid on a bed.

His shoes were pulled off. He knew the laces were being cut, but he could not lift a hand to help. Then his jacket was taken, and his belt undone, and his trousers drawn off, and the covers of the bed were put over him.

A moment later something warm was put at his chest, warm and soft and gurgling, a hot water bottle. Then a pot one was put at his feet, and there was quiet.

Now he felt he could move, and he did manage a little twitch, and then sleep swept up from far away and spread over his brain, and pushed him down into the mattress. He felt himself grow heavier, and then there was nothing.

When he woke he was warm. Dr Wix was sitting beside him, holding his hand. Keith smiled and rubbed his cheeks, which were warm from being slept on.

'You're all right?' said Dr Wix.

'Yes, said Keith, wondering why he was there, and then remembering. 'Where's David?' he said.

Dr Wix looked at him, and opened his mouth to speak. No word came. Keith felt his hand squeezed and then dropped. Dr Wix stood up. Keith saw tears in his eyes and then run on to his cheeks.

'I'm sorry,' said Dr Wix. 'I'm sorry, Keith,' Then he swallowed all his feelings down his throat. 'David's dead,' he said.

'David?' said Keith. 'David.'

'You were both struck by lightning,' said Dr Wix, sitting down again, and once more in control. 'Let's have a look at you, Keith.' And he plugged his ears with the stethoscope.

4

THERE was nothing wrong with Keith, Dr Wix said, but grazes and bruises and slight concussion. He told Keith to stay where he was, because Mrs Watson had said he would be all right there for the night.

'I'll tell your parents,' he said. 'No, don't talk now, just stay where you are and rest. I'll send something up for your headache.'

Keith had not realized he had a headache. Now that Dr Wix told him he felt it like a molten skull clamped over his eyes and down to the nape of his neck, so bad that it seemed to be outside him and not part of him at all. He closed his eyes, and when he opened them again his mother was standing beside him, and had just said his name.

Mrs Watson was going out of the room, having shown her visitor up. His mother spoke again, and Keith could hardly hear what she was saying, because there was a vibration in his ears like a football whistle being blown seven inches away, persistently. He said so. His mother touched his head, laying icy fingers on the hot skin. Keith lay there in the double agony of the two pains. Together they achieved a balance of ecstasy that was bearable between the throbs of his heart, pulsing the pain round his head.

There were white tablets, and peaty water to swallow them down with. Then, later, there was peace, and the pain in his head showed only occasionally, like a black rock sometimes surfacing in the bed of a fast fluctuating river. Then the waters of the drug rose, the rock could be seen but not felt, and a great ease came on him.

He was alone. Downstairs there was the noise of the farm kitchen, the gentle rattle of pots, the antiphony of man and woman speaking, the fire having its throat cleared, and the unplaceable rumblings that come up through the floor to those lying in bed in any house, their own or a strange one. Water pipes gasped and belched, and in from the shippon came the liquid voices and stirrings of cows, and from the yard the fall of the links in the dog's chain.

It was dark. The window was a blue square in a pale wall, where the light from the landing shone through the part open door. Keith stirred, and turned away from the light. The hot water bottle was only as warm as he was now, soft and lifeless at his belly. The one at his feet had gone down to the end of the bed, half a mile away, he thought.

A door opened downstairs, and there was more light. Mrs Watson came up the stairs, and came to look at him. Keith sat up, and asked to visit the bathroom. Then walking was such a dizziness that Mrs Watson had to help him across the bright landing and back again. He got back into a straightened bed, and sat there feeling very blowzy in his vest and underpants and one sock, and a little bit sick after the exertion. Mrs Watson went downstairs and brought him a cup of tea and more of the white tablets.

Frank Watson came up and flopped into bed in the next room with great breathings and gruntings. Mrs Watson said he had gone straight to sleep, but she would be up and about for another hour or two, and would look in again, and leave the landing light on all night. If he wanted anything he had only to call out. Then she went downstairs again. Keith was left with his thoughts, and they were very small ones. He knew there was something he should be thinking about, but all that would present itself was stuff about where his separate limbs were, and how his head was placed, and the softness of the feather mattress under his hip.

He slept again, and woke in the night to hear the outside air shocking the window; and then he woke in daylight to hear rain hissing on the moor and the kettle boiling downstairs.

He got up, finding his clothes on the chair by the bed, washed, and walked downstairs, and sat by the fire. There was no one in the kitchen.

Frank Watson came in with steam rising from his hat and water dripping from it, and cigarette smoke lying like grey knitting round him in the still air.

'Are you right?' he said.

'No so bad,' said Keith.

'Mother,' called Frank, and Mrs Watson came in from the back of the house, drying her hands on her apron.

'We let you lie,' she said. 'Will you have an egg now?'

'Yes please,' said Keith, when he had considered himself, and the fire had struck through and dried him from the surrounding wet air.

'You'll be needing something,' said Frank Watson. Then they both looked at him in a way he didn't understand. Keith suddenly felt a stranger, and Mrs Watson saw that they had upset him a little.

'You're welcome here, you know,' she said. 'And so would David Wix be welcome, if it was possible.'

'I know about him,' said Keith. 'Isn't he here?'

'No,' said Frank Watson, and again he hesitated in his thoughts. 'You were knocked senseless,' he said.

'I know that David was. . . . That he was there too,' said Keith. 'Dr Wix told me. Did he take him home?'

'We weren't meant to tell you anything,' said Mrs Watson. 'But you're asking, isn't he, Frank?'

'It's worse than you know,' said Frank Watson.

'David isn't there at all,' said Mrs Watson. 'When Frank got to you there was only you. David disappeared.'

'I saw the lightning and came straight over,' said Frank Watson. 'There was only you.'

'Then I can't even see him,' said Keith. 'I can't even see him at all.'

'Not you, or us, or Dr Wix himself,' said Mrs Watson. 'And there's Dr Wix alone now, first his wife, and now his son; and what'll he do?'

'Never mind that,' said Frank Watson. 'There's one here will want his breakfast.'

'I'll do that,' said Mrs Watson; and Keith sat by the fire stupefied. But he was able to eat his egg, and bread and marmalade, from a shop jar and hollow eating compared with the rare home-made sort.

Frank Watson went out and finished his outside jobs. Mrs Watson finished washing the eggs, and then tidied round Keith. She told him his father would come up soon to take him home. The morning church bells sounded up the valley from the town, in irrelevant requiem to the vanished David.

Frank Watson came in and started talking about cows and sheep, which were nothing much to Keith's fancy. Yet they were better than the ceaseless circling thought that David was not only dead but lost too. Frank sat opposite him, and offered him a cigarette. Keith took one, and lit it, and found the smoke soothed him until it was bitter half-way down. Then he let it go out.

'You haven't taken to it much, then,' said Frank. Keith said he hadn't. But his mind was running more easily now. He asked about the boggart, because he had heard nothing of it all night or this morning.

'That fellow,' said Frank Watson. 'I settled him yesterday, when I'd brought you in. He'd been making a to-do-ment about the spot, and he was getting into a right old tear, moving the table about and throwing the chairs over. So I turned and gave him a right cussing. But that only set him off worse. So I thought, mebbe I'm a sinful man, mebbe I never go to church or chapel, and mebbe I'm no better than the next man. But I'm God's creature, which is more than that fellow is, so I stood there and lifted my hand and said "Christ and his angels and God himself and the Holy Ghost be upon you and remove from this place to do evil in another place, where there's folks that don't mind, Amen", and there was silence like you never heard, and the table put back, and the chairs picked up; and, God help me, he's out there with my wife scrubbing eggs like a Christian. And there's me wondering what sort of a sin I've done.'

'I don't know,' said Keith. 'What sort of sin did David do, to get taken away like that?'

'Never question the ways of God,' said Frank. 'It's more than we know.'

'Perhaps it wasn't God that took him,' said Keith. 'Did it look like God?'

'It looked like lightning to me,' said Frank. 'But I can hear a car coming, and that's your father, I doubt.'

It was Mr Heseltine, coming up with a taxi. Whilst the taxi turned in the yard he thanked Mr and Mrs Watson. Then he and Keith went out into the rain and into the car, and went in silence down the lane, and into the shining streets and home.

After lunch Dr Wix came and looked at him. He said he was all right, but ought to take things quietly for a day or two, but he could go to school if he wanted. No games for the time being, and he would have a word with Dr Tate himself, to see that he understood. Keith's father said he would do that. Dr Wix said he would have to go to the school in any case. Then he went out quietly, saying he had more patients to see, and didn't really want to be entertained for the time being. Work, he said, was best for him now.

The rain stopped. The sun came out, but not strongly enough to raise a mist. The day grew less heavy. Keith took two more of the tablets, to submerge the headache that was lifting its reef again. He waited until the healing tide ran smooth over the pain, and then went for a gentle walk.

His way took him to the town end of Hare Trod. It was where he had meant to go, but not really where he had wanted his feet to take him. He met no one in the town, and only a country bus passed him, lathered with mud from the lanes, the gills of its windows steamed solid.

He walked up Hare Trod. Water ran on the land and

along the levels of the path. The sunlight began to die, because the sun itself sank behind the hills. The moon hung round in the sky, no lighter than its surroundings yet, just an object, a mere latitude of heaven, no lantern.

Sheep grazed. In the well-trodden places where the Trod crossed a wall there was water lying in the strange topography of the cow-trodden mud, a finely filtered sea bed under the surface. Beyond the second ridge, coming nearer to the spot where the thing had happened, he saw someone, walking about. It was no giant, but a man in a peaked cap, dark against the hill.

It was the policeman he knew, looking at the ground. Keith walked up the path to him, and stood watching.

'You shouldn't be up here,' said the policeman, with no touch of authority in his voice, only sympathy.

'This is the place,' said Keith, and his voice lost itself on the hillside.

'Aye, but not the place for you, lad,' said the policeman. 'Don't you think I'd better take you home?'

Keith looked at the ground. There was no sign of anything strange here at all. There was only the level sheep pasture, and the Trod dinting it. There was no mark to indicate that here David had died in a way that Keith himself had only just begun to realize. To him it had been a black line, to Frank Watson it had been lightning. Whatever it had been, it had taken David; and never again would he walk here with him, never again talk to him or see him, or hold any traffic of conversation with him. He had gone, as the drummer boy had gone, and unless some future time brought him out again, he was gone for ever.

'I will go,' he said, and turned. He saw the whole world empty before him, the town smoke showing beyond the next ridge, and nothing left in it for him, now that David had been pulled out from it. All at once he knew what it had felt like to be a lost being in a strange world, what it had felt like to be Nellie Jack John, and why David had been so careful with him and for him. He understood, now that his face was put against it, what David had known by instinct, that the lost places are in this world and belong to the people in it and are all that they have to call home.

A wave of physical sorrow came to him, and he went on his knees and covered his face, though that would not hide it. It did not hide the sobs that came now, and the tears that sprang against his will from his tissues, out from his body like earthquakes. The policeman stood by making a comforting noise, and urging him to stand up with a hand under his arm. Keith stood, at last, and the policeman led him down the hill, and to his house, empty of everything, and new.

5

NOBODY called Keith the next morning. He woke to the day lying in front of him, open for ever, boundless and flat, without the civil divisions of school to regulate it. His mother was downstairs, busy with the work of the house. The church clock was sounding quarter to nine, and the daylight was bright over the Cleveland Hills.

The eight-fifty train bravo'd a bit at the curve leaving the station, and then chuntered down the line. Keith lay where he was for a moment, considering things. He thought he would go to school, because that would keep his mind busy, or if not busy, it would at least limit his vision. And he did not want to see very far today, or ever, perhaps. All the view of life he had seemed directed to the past, and nothing to the future, and very little to the actual present, the actual sitting up in bed, holding his toes, yawning, heaving his feet over the side of the bed, standing up and putting on his slippers: none of these actions seemed to be happening in full fact. They each seemed without illumination, like a scale model of the event they were imitating, like a dull carving of the present.

His mother came up to see what he was thinking of doing. She thought he should stay in bed and nurse his headache; but he had no headache now, only an emptiness behind the eyes; and that, he thought, was due to the hurricane that had gone through him and left him all disordered, but undamaged.

He was late to school, of course, but he knew that would not matter, except that he would have to report to the kitchen so that there was a dinner for him. Even that was not vital, because there was always more dinner than people needed, and vats of it went out to be reconverted at the piggery. Now it would be at some other piggery, since the one here was still empty.

Prayers and morning assembly had not finished. Keith waited outside for the singing to stop, with seven Roman Catholics, a Jew, and a Professed Atheist. The Professed Atheist was in Keith's own form, and had given up God a term ago, and was allowed to miss the prayers. He was a conscientious objector to prayers, he had told Dr Tate. Dr Tate wanted to know where his conscience had derived from, in that case, but the Professed Atheist had said his logic was weaker than his convictions, and had declined to argue. Dr Tate had called him a Convicted Atheist for a few days, and then left him alone, saying that Religious Freedom and Irreligious Freedom were sometimes the same thing.

The door opened, and the Other Denominations crept in to their places at the back of the hall.

'Before the announcements,' said Dr Tate, 'I have

some news of a particularly horrifying nature. It is not the sort of thing I like to make public remarks about, but I think it is best to inform everybody so that you know what you're gossiping about. On Saturday afternoon Wix and Heseltine K. were walking on Hare Trod. Without any warning, and contrary to the weather signs, they were struck by lightning. There is no doubt of it, because it was seen to happen by two independent witnesses. Heseltine K. was knocked out, bruised and concussed, but not otherwise hurt; but Wix was killed. You may sit down if you want.'

There had been some stirring in the ranks before him. Each person there had heard already about David's death, but this was the first time authority had spoken about it, and the first time this particular authority had addressed them with such blunt words. His usual blunt homilies were about school morale and discipline, verging on the abusive, and admonitory. This talk about Wix, whom they had seen on Friday, being killed the next day made them move uncomfortably. It was almost as if Dr Tate were announcing his execution for tomorrow, or later the same day.

'He was not only killed,' Dr Tate went on, 'but the force of the lightning was such that he was vaporized instantly, and there is no trace of him. There is nothing left at all. Those are the facts about Wix. I must tell you that it has been almost beyond me to stand here and tell you about this almost incomprehensible accident. I do not know, for instance, of any event like it. Before I talk more about Wix himself there are one or two other points. First, there will in course of time be an inquest. There always is in the case of sudden death. The inquest cannot be held without the authority of the Home Secretary, because there is no body. Now, this is a spectacular affair, and there will be great public interest, and a great many people will be present, out of a natural curiosity, and some out of unnatural curiosity. I do not wish any of you to be there. There is no need for you to be, and there will be a full and accurate account of the proceedings in the local paper, and possibly in some of the national papers. Your interest can be satisfied by reading those reports. Only a nasty and ignorant curiosity would take you to the inquest itself. The next thing is that you may be approached by members of the press for information about Wix, and your recollections of him, and things like that. Will you please refer all such requests to me, personally. I respect the press, I think it for the most part chooses its words wisely and stays within the bounds of proper behaviour. But there have been instances the other way. If you send reporters and journalists to me I will do all I can to help them. We do not want the wrong kind of shadow to fall on the school, and the wrong kind of background to the country's view of David Wix.

'The next point is a little more difficult. Heseltine K, Keith Heseltine, was with Wix at the time, and suffered a nasty banging about. . . . No limbs were broken, but at first it was thought his skull was fractured, because of certain bleeding from his nose and ears. But that is believed to be due to air pressure in the region of the electric discharge. He was, however, deliriously unconscious for some time afterwards. Now, after a shock, and in such conditions, any of you might talk about anything. Heseltine talked about giants and supernatural events, the details of which I don't know and wouldn't go into if I did. But the thing I want to put across is that it would be unmannerly and cruel, possibly vicious, of you if you were to tease him about anything he said in the state of shock he was in. Some of the things he said may be reported at the inquest. I want you to remember that the things he then thought were real were no more than dreams, the dreams we all have. The electric shock has possibly fixed them in that part of the mind that is looked on as holding memories. He may remember things that did not happen. We will do our best to make him forget them. He will not be at school this week. By that time we shall have stopped gossiping about the affair. And now I will talk about David Wix.'

And he did. Keith could bear to hear about himself, he could bear hearing that he had babbled of giants, he could bear to hear that his memory was imaginary. He knew it wasn't. It was impossible, he thought, for memories of what he and David had done to be altered so much, and be so clear and well ordered. It was, after all, David who had seen the giants first. But to hear about David was too much. He opened the door behind him and crawled out of the hall, and went home.

His mother was glad to see him, and told him he looked tired. He sat in the kitchen all the morning, and let the world become slowly more actual and fit to be considered. After dinner he slept for a little while, which surprised him very much, because sleeping in daylight was a thing he hardly ever did.

The daylight was lessening when he woke. His mind was easier now, and he thought of a way of proving to himself that the giants were no trick of memory, that they were real. He had a cup of tea, and then went up to Dr Wix's house.

There was one light on there. He let himself in at the back door, as usual, and found Dr Wix taking his own tea in his study, where he and David had often played chess.

'How are you?' said Dr Wix. 'A professional visit?'

'Just a visit,' said Keith. 'I wanted to come, even if David wasn't here.'

'I'll just take a quick look,' said Dr Wix, and he flashed

his little light into Keith's eyes in turn, asked him about headaches, and then offered him more tea, ringing the bell for a cup to be brought.

Keith drank the tea. 'I went to school this morning,' he said.

'You shouldn't have,' said Dr Wix.

'I came away,' said Keith. 'I only went to assembly. Dr Tate was talking about things. He talked about things I said when I was unconscious.'

'I was going to tell you about that,' said Dr Wix. 'The mind has its images. Look at the myths of ancient Greece and the Welsh tales, and the Norse Gods, and the Hindu stories, and just think of the mythologies we don't know. Well, they're all very similar. Your ravings, well, they weren't ravings, exactly, but strange talk, were on the same lines, the figures the mind uses, giants and things like that. Rather convincing, but nothing to worry about.'

'Can I go up to David's room?' said Keith. 'I want to get something?'

Dr Wix said he might go up at any time. Keith went up, and found the room doubly empty. It would have been less empty if it had been changed, but it was the same as it always had been, with even the two marks on the bed where they had both sat on Saturday morning.

He found the book they had begun to write, and took it downstairs with him. He did not want to bother with the first part, about the drummer boy. He wanted to find what notes David had made in the back.

He found what he wanted. There, in David's handwriting, with a date as the heading, was a note that they had seen a giant on the fell side, walking up out of Vendale.

'Oh,' said Dr Wix, turning the pages. He read the cutting David had put there, about the Jingle Stones, and glanced at the list of words that Nellie Jack John had used. 'Keith,' he said, 'there is something strange going on. I am quite prepared to believe that Frank Watson's boggart is a natural phenomenon that we know very little about. But this notebook leads me to suppose there are supernatural phenomena we don't know about. And I am just wondering whether I am mad to think that perhaps David is not. . . .' But he did not finish what he was saying. He shook his head, and gave the book back to Keith. 'I must go to my evening surgery,' he said.

Keith went out of the back door. There was something else he wanted besides the notebook. The notebook had proved the giant was no faulty memory. He could in fact, he thought, bear any amount of teasing now, without feeling it was cruel.

He went into the shed in the yard and picked up the tin with the candle in. The pale gleam was still inside, and the tin was cold in his hand.

It was dark as he went home, and more than dark. There should have been a moon, but there was a great obscurity overhead, and no star showed. There was a thickness in the air, so that no distance showed along the ground either. He walked in darkness, and felt he was part of it.

He was almost home, just turning the corner to cross the road, when the darkness solidified in front of him and brought him to a stop. There was nothing there but an abstract arrest. He was halted on the pavement. He felt foolish, because if anyone had seen him stop they would have wondered what he was doing. He found he was leaning on an enclosing cushion that invisibly kept him where he was.

He had not time to collect his thoughts enough to be frightened. There was a twitch in the thickness of the dark, a pale yellow-green movement in front of him, and the tin holding the candle had fallen from his hands to the pavement, and clanged there once.

Something moved away very rapidly. It was not so much a going away as a re-ordering of the darkness. There was nothing to see, it was more like an invisible and inaudible precipitation or crystallization in some compound. The resistance went from the night, and he could move, but there was the feeling that there had been a chemical change in the darkness.

He picked up the tin, which had not opened, and went into the house, looking back at the other side of the road before he closed the door. There was nothing to see. The reaction, whatever it was, was over. He took the tin upstairs, looked in it once, and set the candle upright, and put it behind books on a shelf, and the notebook in front of it, and went down to supper.

6

KEITH woke in the night with the chill hand of some internal terror stroking his heart. He sat up and breathed air that seemed warm and dry of oxygen and without nourishment. The physical spasm passed, but the terror stayed in his mind for a time, subsiding gradually to something different, something quite a long way, in fact, from terror. It was as if something worked in his mind from outside, trying to turn his thoughts towards something, in a way that was not kindly; a sort of mental bullying. Then that went too, and only its memory stayed. Some memories bring back with them the feeling associated with them; extreme heights numb the feet, and slipping on wet cobbles and going down is remembered with a tingling of the elbows that reached the ground first. But this memory was like one remembered from being written down, not from being experienced. When the event had gone Keith looked back and saw it almost as if it had been on the page.

In the morning it was still there. As a memory it held no more terror. It was merely a puzzle. Why should he have felt anything at all? He disengaged his mind from it, and considered the two choices for the day.

They were more than choices. They were both temptations, because either would suit him. To go to school or to stay at home. There seemed to be no urgency about going to school, and no drawbacks to staying at home.

He found it had been decided for him. He heard the eight-fifty train leave the station, and decided not to rush to school. Instead he went to sleep again.

When he was up an hour later, and having his breakfast while his mother vacuumed the stairs, a third temptation came to him. It was like nothing he had ever felt before. He almost obeyed it without thinking. He had an urge to go up to his room and bring out the box with the candle in, and gaze on the flame. The thought filled his mind, and for a moment he thought of nothing else. It was something he had to do, and the desire to do it came on him like a storm. He dropped a piece of toast, and stood up.

But at that moment the kettle for his tea boiled over. When he had dealt with that the urge to look at the candle flame had gone. He looked back on it with the same detachment as he had looked at the terror in the night. They were the same thing: both had been imposed on him from outside himself. They were not things that rose out of his own being. The candle flame was unlucky, at the very least, he thought. David had gazed at it, and afterwards had seemed to see things, or seen ordinary things differently. It had an effect that was not good. But it had been like David to be full of obscure enthusiasms,

145

and perceptions that seemed almost not real to others. That he had looked at the flame was one thing; but Keith himself had no reason for any feelings about it.

But for all that, there it was upstairs now; and the other thing that he could do with it was lose it where he could never possibly look at it again. But even that he wouldn't bother to do.... He had no feelings, as he drank his tea, either way for the candle.

Later in the day, when he was in the market place, taking the air and buying toffees, the strong sudden urge came again. He turned and hurried towards home, without toffees. Then he came in sight of the house, and the desire failed again. He shook his head and wondered what he had been about. Shaking his head brought back the slight headache that had been with him since Saturday, now and then. He kept still, and it went. He turned round and went back to the shops, and bought toffees. His mother was a marvel at jam, but no good at toffee at all.

The candle called him twice a day after that, at odd times. He grew used to it. The first three or four times he started up and went to where the tin was, but the call died as he did so. Then he knew the feeling as it came, and let it wash over him. He had to, in fact, because once he was in the bus, and another time in church, and a third time in assembly.

Then, one evening the call came again, when he was in his room. Nothing prevented him from walking over to the shelf and taking the tin down, opening it, and standing the waxy candle on the table, putting out the electric light, and looking at the little wand of pale flame spinning steadily on its wick. As he looked he saw the movement. He might have been looking at some spindly molecule.

Then the call went. The flame was now a flame, of

strange and uncertain nature, perhaps, but there seemed to be in his mind no reason for looking into it. He dropped the candle into its box, put on the electric light, went out into the garden, and found a spade, shovelled up the edge of a dug vegetable bed, and dropped the tin in, and smoothed the earth over it.

The next morning he had the tin out again, because the irresistible impulse came on him when he was in the garden, and his thoughts were resting and unguarded. He looked on the flame in daylight, and saw the world's light grow less round him, and that of the candle grow whiter and whiter, until he was looking into a cave of light. Suddenly he found he was unwilling to look further, and took his eyes from it. The pale sky over the garden came into his landscape again, wrinkled and withered with cloud, and the gem of the candle flame winked like a complete star between his thumbs. He dropped the candle into the tin, and heeled it into the ground again.

There were shadows with him during the day, as if there were small clouds just out of sight behind the things he was looking at; strange atomic assemblies behind doors and blackboards, things just hidden behind settees and buses, more people present than the room really held. But those were phantoms from his own eyes, he knew. They were all tinged with green, and that must be the reflex of the candle flame, like the colour that stains a white wall after looking at a coloured object, the complementary of what has been seen.

Then he stayed away from the garden, and began to fight back at the assailing temptation. By standing still he could outlast it, but the usual way of overcoming was no good. Whilst the urge was on him he could not by any means think of anything else. All he could think of was going or not going.

The inquest came about a month after David's death. It was held on a Friday afternoon, during school time. Keith had to go, because he was a principal witness. He went up the steps of the Town Hall with Dr Wix, and they were both very grave.

There was a knot of men at the top of the steps, looking down at whoever came in. Among them there was a sudden scuffle, as if a slow dance had begun at the centre of the group. Then there was a sudden flood of light low down, flowing over the floor and down the steps and illuminating a frieze of legs. Then the group parted to let Keith and Dr Wix go by. Keith heard a hissing whisper, saying that it was the act of a fool to take flash photographs of boys who have been struck by lightning.

The Town Hall was full. The people there did not seem, as Dr Tate had thought, to be ignorant and inquisitive, but to be there out of some duty. The duty was probably sympathy for Dr Wix, who passed through the ranked chairs to the front with his head bowed rather. He and Keith were shown to chairs by the policeman Keith knew, the one who had comforted him and brought him down from the moor.

Mr Sydney Wadham, the Coroner, came in. There was some confusion among the people about whether they should stand or not. But Mr Wadham did not give them much chance to dither. He sat down and looked at them all.

Frank Watson was just leaning over from his chair behind Keith to say, 'How are you framing', and Mr Wadham gave him a look that stopped him. Then he wriggled his mouth, as if he were putting his lower jaw into place, and started to speak.

'This is an inquest into the death of David Francis Wix, of this town, on the nineteenth of October this year.' He then settled his jaw more firmly, wrote on a

148

piece of paper, and went on to explain that there was no jury at this sort of inquiry, that the delay was due to the necessity of applying to the Home Secretary for leave to hold an inquest, and that he hoped to have the proceedings over in the shortest possible space of time, call Constable Hunter.

Constable Hunter was Keith's friend. He said that he was called to Swang on the day in question, following reports of an occurrence on the moor. When he got there he found one boy unconscious, to wit, Keith Heseltine, and no trace of any other. Following conversation with Mr Frank Watson and another person. . . . And there the Coroner wanted to know who the other person was. The Constable said he had not been able to ascertain the other person's name, but the said person was present as a witness. The Coroner asked him to continue. The Constable said that he had noted what the witnesses had said, and then proceeded to a certain spot on the moor, on the path known as Hare Trod and made investigations. When he was asked what the results were (with another bedding in of the jaw) he said they were without result. There had been nothing to make the area any different from the rest of the path. He had formed no suspicions.

'Thank you, Constable,' said Mr Wadham. 'No suspicions of any kind?'

'None in relation to the matter before us now, Sir,' said the Constable, and was allowed to step down.

'Are you in any hurry, Dr Wix?' said the Coroner. 'I can take your evidence as soon as you like.'

'I should like to stay, in any case,' said Dr Wix. 'I am at your convenience.'

Frank Watson was next, rather nervous. The Coroner called him, and then studied a paper on his table, looked very seriously at Frank, and jerked his jaw twice.

'Frank Harold Watson,' he said. 'What have you to

say? You understand that I shall have to ask you certain questions at the end of your evidence, in view of the statement you have already given to the police.'

'Aye,' said Frank. 'That I do.' Then he stated that he had been in the field adjoining the moor when Keith and David had walked along the Trod. They had previously been at his house. At this point he grew more nervous than ever, and turned to look at his wife, who looked at the floor. The Coroner told him to go on. Frank said that there had been a disturbance among the sheep, and he had put that down to the boggart. At this point the Coroner said he must issue a stern warning, in fact two stern warnings. One was to the witness to stick to the literal truth, since he was on oath, and a responsible citizen, and a Rural District Councillor at that. The other warning was to the public, that any noise would result in the clearing of the court. Meanwhile, as he had already said, the witness must stick to facts. Frank said that there had been a boggart at Swang for centuries, and that recently, after a long sleep, it had come into activity again, and caused a number of mishaps. The Coroner said that it was with great reluctance he noted the so-called facts down, and would the witness proceed slowly, since all his notes had to be taken down in longhand. He would ask the witness to sign them, if he insisted that they were a true record, later. Frank went on to say that the sheep quietened, and he was leading them down the field, looking at the two boys, who were going down the path known as Hare Trod. The sky had darkened suddenly, like an eclipse, and there had been a violent flash of lightning and a clap of thunder. He had seen one of the boys, Keith Heseltine, thrown down, and ran to the place to see how they had fared. He was only able to find one boy. Of the other, David Wix, there was no sign at all. No Sir, he could not have run away in any direction, there was no time. No Sir, he did not attribute the lightning to the boggart, and would not like to have it thought at fault in any way, and if the Coroner would be good enough to call Mrs Watson, well, she would prove it.

'I think you had better come up here and sign this now, Mr Watson,' said the Coroner, setting his jaw to one side as he wrote the last words. Frank Watson went to his table, had the testimony read to him in a low voice, and signed it.

Mrs Watson was called next. She said she was the wife of Frank Watson, of Swang, and on the day in question the two boys had visited the farm. They were on friendly terms, and one of them was their doctor's son and the other a relative. Shortly after they had left, Mrs Watson had been in the kitchen. She had just placed a pan of water on the fire, to warm for washing up some cooking things. No, there was no hot water supply at the farm. She had no sooner put the water on than there was a puff of smoke out of the chimney, and the water began to boil, or appear to. She went to tend to it, and as she bent over there was a flash of light outside the window, followed by a clap of thunder. She lifted the pan off the fire, and it went on boiling, with water splashing out of it on to the hearth. The water that splashed out turned immediately to ice. The water in the pan remained very cold. She was sure that the boggart had fallen down the chimney into it, and she was sure that it had fallen before the thunder. It was a nervous creature. After a time, and before her husband brought Keith Heseltine in, the boggart had got out of the water and started playing heck. Well, playing war.

Would Mrs Watson mind signing the statement she had just made? Mrs Watson was glad to.

'I am sure that some of the things we are discussing will sound strange to some of the people here,' said Mr

Wadham. 'But we are dealing with what is in any case an almost unique event. Lightning is only one degree removed from the supernatural in any case; and if we are going to talk about boggarts we might as well have the whole truth about them. Would Dr Richard David Wix take the stand?'

Dr Wix said that he had last seen his son at lunch-time on the day in question. He had seemed his usual self, but he had not looked at him with a clinical eye. They said, did they not, that the cobbler's child was the worst shod? No Sir, he did not mean that there was anything ailing with his son, nor had he complained of anything, even trivial. He had gone for a walk with Keith Heseltine, without stating where he was going. There was no sign of thunder in the air when he left. Yes, witness had heard a clap of thunder during the afternoon. He had later been called to Swang and seen Keith Heseltine. No Sir, Keith Heseltine had made no conscious statement, but during a delirium, following shock, he had talked of legendary beings. Giants, in fact, Sir. He had not mentioned boggarts. Yes, the witness had observed a manifestation at Swang. He had previously been called to attend Mrs Watson, who had been hurt by the boggart. Yes, he was quite sure the boggart existed. He did not think there was any link between the lightning and the boggart. Yes Sir, he would gladly sign his statement.

The next witness refused to give his name. He was a little red-faced man with brown eyes that stuck out. He said that he had been on the edge of the moor that day with a wheelbarrow, stealing turf. No Sir, not peat, sods with the grass still on, for his garden. Yes, he realized that he need not give evidence that incriminated him. He was willing to be charged with the offence of stealing turf, but would not give his name. No Sir, he lived fifty miles away, and had brought his car to take the turf away.

At that point Constable Hunter spoke to the Coroner, who then assured the witness that no action was to be taken against him, and commended him on the public spirit he was showing in laying himself open to prosecution by coming here today. The witness then said that he had laid low when he saw two boys walking down the edge of the moor, and was watching them when they were struck down. Immediately before the lightning it had been his impression that something came flying down from the sky over their heads, and that one boy had raised his hands to it and spoken. No he had not been able to distinguish the words. The boy was not in court. He concluded that ... The Coroner said his conclusions were not needed, and what had come flying down from the sky? The witness said it was a man on horseback, and not so much flying as seeming to be galloping down a hill.

The Coroner required his signature, and said he might leave at once, since he was travelling by bus, and he hoped that his public spirit in one matter would cancel out the moral debility shown in his stealing of turf and that he would be now neither better nor worse that he had been before. The witness left.

Keith was next. He said that they had been to the Jingle Stones, after reading an unfinished paragraph in the paper. He named the paper. The Coroner did something with his face that could have been a smile: you would have to know him to be sure. They had visited Swang. They had both seen a disturbance in the sheep. They had both met the boggart. Yes, met was a good way of putting it. David Wix had some sort of power over it. Yes, they had both seen giants, some weeks before, and he had seen a note in David's writing about them. No, he had not seen lightning himself, only a gap in the sky. David had said something about a butterfly, and raised his hands. Witness had then recovered consciousness hanging over Frank Watson's back. His headaches were better now.

The Coroner made him stand down. Then he said that some of the witnesses had attested to strange things that afternoon. Some of them were beyond his province, but for all that they had been very properly brought to notice, and he was glad that the witnesses had been bold enough to say what they had. But nothing they had said had altered the plainest fact of all, that David Francis Wix had met his death by being struck by lightning, and so he would record it. Then he shut his mouth and let his jaw hang.

'Come this way,' said Frank Watson. 'We don't want to be in with these fellows at the back. They're from the paper.' And he led them out of the door the Coroner had used, into the Ladies Cloakroom, down a staircase, into a passage, and into an ironmonger's shop, coming out among hanging shopping baskets and wire plate racks, the smell of naphthalene fire lighters and paint brushes. So they got away without being questioned.

Part Four

FIRE AND FLEET AND
CANDLELIGHT

I

KEITH walked up with Dr Wix and stayed to tea before the surgery began. It was a quiet little meal, and it was almost like going out to visit politely some one of Keith's relatives, of whom he had many, who had perhaps not seen him since he was two years old, and whom he could not remember. On these occasions there would be either a good many hearty instructions to 'Reach to', or minute passings of minute cake and sandwiches no bigger than the diagrams to theorems in geometry books, and somewhat of the same shape; and often with the filling so much stacked in the middle that only by biting and swallowing could Keith say to himself Q.E.D., which had to be shown.

But Dr Wix's tea was an absent-minded one between equals. He drank a cup, refilled Keith's cup, waved at the food, and said 'I'm glad that's over. There has to be something public on these occasions. And there can't be a funeral.'

'There's sometimes a service,' said Keith.

'Not this time, somehow,' said Dr Wix. 'A public ceremony of some kind is called for, and that's all. We've had that. At the end of the year I shall resign, and at the end of March I shall leave – I have to give three months' notice, you see. Then I think I shall go to Australia, where even the landscape is different. But I'm not saying anything to anyone else about it until much nearer the time. I don't want to carry on here for ever, for another twenty years until I retire.'

'I've got fifty years until I retire,' said Keith.

'Don't start working it out like that at your age,' said

Dr Wix. 'I'm sure that your fifty years doesn't look any longer than my twenty, for all that.' Then he took his black notebook and started to enter his calls.

Keith left at the beginning of the surgery, and walked down through the town, thinking that today he had come to the last page of a book, turned it, and found the blank leaves at the end, without even advertisements on. Something was over and done with, he thought. Life was now another book, a fresh one, unopened, only unlike real books in that he couldn't turn on a few pages and see what it was going to be like, or even look at the last chapter to see whether there was a happy ending, or even whether the last pages had anything printed on them at all.

He was revolving the idea in his mind, and wondering after all whether the book was printed, whether the liver of the life wrote it as he went, when he turned a corner, out of the lights of the market place, into the dark of a Wynd, and was brought to a standstill.

It was not the first time he had been stopped like this. There had been a time a few nights ago when he had been walking home, the last time he had been to Dr Wix's house, and a thickening of darkness had held him. Here again was the thickening of the dark, the same presence in front. But this time there was more to it than last time.

'Look where you're going,' said a voice, over his head.

'Get a light on it,' said Keith, waking up to where he was, and dismissing for the moment the similar idea that had come into his mind.

He had walked into a horse, a horse with a rider. It was a real horse, with the smell and the warmth and the movement of reality, but the invisibility of another world. On the horse was a girl. If there was a horse, he thought, there was usually a girl on it. David had said

that they rode them to make up for being ugly themselves. Keith had not been able to agree that that was a
motive, but he had concluded that it was a result. This
girl he could not see. The horse had its shoulder against
him. It turned its head, and he saw its eye reflecting the
lights of the market place. He stepped back, and went
round the creature.

'Did he tread on your feet?' said the girl.

'No,' said Keith. 'Is he trained to?'

'Don't be so soft,' said the girl, and talked to the horse,
soothing it as if it had had a lion walk into it, not Keith.

There is a feeling that comes at times, that what is going on has happened before, and that if things would
stop for a moment you would be able to prophesy the
next event. Keith had that feeling, and more, at this moment. Instead of fading into the junk heap where dreams
lie, it was growing into something more actual. The act
of prophecy evaded him, though, but the parallel with
the time when there was no horse grew more and more
obvious to him, and he could now no longer understand
why he had not known the first time that it was a horse.
And the man who would give no name, who had seen a
horse with a rider, added his word from memory. What
Keith had walked into on the corner on the night he was
carrying the candle home was a horse, without smell or
warmth or movement, but a horse. The shoulder had
stood against him in the same way, the head had come
round and been over his own shoulder in the same way:
the two situations balanced.

But to Keith there had come no death and no lightning. There was no crack in the sky, no butterfly, or
thing like one, no flash, no disappearance. He was still
here.

Then there came the pulse of whatever it was that
drew him to the candle; and he knew he must go to it. It

was, somehow, now calling him on its own now. He himself wanted to know what it wanted with him. He was no longer being called without knowing whether there was a reason. Now, at least, he knew there was a reason, but what it was, and how he would learn, he did not know.

He looked back down the Wynd. The horse had gone. But not by any loss of chemical tension. It had simply walked away. He could hear it on the cobbles. Something real had brought him near to something unreal.

He went into the garden before going into the house. The top layer of the earth was like cardboard with the frost. He kicked it, and broke its hold, then lifted the corrugation away, and dug the cold soil with his hands. He pulled at the tin, but it had stuck, because the cold influence of the flame had set the frost lower here and bound it into the earth. The lid came open, and the tiny fluorescence glittered against the ground. He picked the candle up, and walked into the house with it, and it was as if something inside him and something outside him too, had waited for this time, when he would be neither hurried, nor forced, but ready to look into the flame and see what was there, and what had taken David.

2

KEITH woke early in the morning, before it was light outside. It was light in his room, where the candle filled all the space with its lucency, steady as the sun. He had woken with a thought in his mind, something that he should have known before, should have thought long ago.

'Slow-witted,' he said to himself, for the sake of company, staring at the candle at the other side of the room. The candle stared back. The window was cold and dark in the wall.

Keith reviewed the thought. It was a simple one, now it was here. The man on the horse, the horse that was invisible, the real horse that reminded him of the invisible one, all related back to Nellie Jack John, through the thing that David had noticed first about him. Nellie Jack John had gone into the castle hill to look for treasure. But the treasure had a history, and belonged to someone. Or at least, it did if you thought there was any treasure. Even if you didn't think there was treasure there was still the owner of it in the hill: King Arthur; and one of the notable things about King Arthur was the fact that he rode a horse, and used it in fighting.

So the man on horseback, when David was taken into the crack in the world, might have been King Arthur. Keith stopped looking at anything in particular, and thought to himself that he was gradually waking up, and that when he was fully awake the idea would grow pale and vanish.

He got out of bed and stood by the window, to wake himself up, looking out into the night. There was so much light in the room that he had to put his hands round his eyes to see through the glass. Otherwise all he saw was the room again, with himself looking in, or out. The idea still persisted, that King Arthur had been the cause of the man riding the horse.

There was not complete darkness outside. There was a patch of light in the garden. Keith thought it was from a downstairs window, and wondered who had left the light on. Then he moved, and saw a shadow move too. The patch of light was from his own window, and was cast by the candle. He stood still, wiped breath from the window, and looked out at the patch of light.

The patch of light still moved. It was not the light it-self moving on the ground, but something moving within the patch of light, like mist. Yet it was not mist. It had too much shape to be mere mist, too much alive-ness, even though it did not move so much as mist might. It moved as if it were alive, and at the same time it was not quite canny, and not quite observable.

Keith lifted the window, and found he was very cold indeed. He held it open, ready to pull it down again at once if he had to. He thought there might be interference in the glass, his own breath perhaps throwing figures on to the light.

But the movement was still there. Keith did not want to think of the thing he was almost sure he could see: a horseman.

There was something more than fancy involved. He turned away from the window, thinking of switching on the light. Then he thought that would be too severe, and brought the candle instead, and held it out into the dewy early morning, and saw what was there.

The light struck out across the garden, across the gar-dens to either side, across the world beyond, and seemed to show like a moon-day to the distant hills. And in its light there was an army standing, transparently smoky green, standing and moving, and all encamped against the house. And they were all as real as himself. They were set, somehow, against the grain of the world, so that Keith himself felt slightly as if he were leaning. It was like being in a deceptive house in a fairground, where you can hardly walk on what appears flat, and when you are given a marble and set it down, it runs up the sloping floor and then up the wall and out of the window. That was the only strain on Keith at the mo-ment. There was no doubt of the actuality of the things he saw. They stood as if they were held, like iron filings, and prickly like them too, against a different force from the one that held Keith to the house and the floor of the world.

There were horsemen and walking men, flags and fires, and out in the plain apparitions in the same focus with the same intensity, distant, yet close against his eyes. It was as if a picture were being shone on the sky by the candle.

Then the things outside seemed to have no meaning any more. They did not fade from sight, only from significance. They suddenly had no more meaning. It was like the last cup of tea you needed: the teapot was laid aside until next time. It no longer held any promises.

Keith closed the window on what was there, put the candle down, and went back to bed.

He was woken, as he often was, by the early train. He looked from the window into a grey rainy morning, and saw nothing but the station and the lighted carriages threading their way along the track, and the dismal plume rising from the exhausts of the diesel motors, to be swamped by the rain and break up in the wake of the train.

There was no school today. It was the sort of day that David would have woken up. There would have been something in it for him. For Keith there was only the feeling of cold, damp air over everything, and the landscape closed in by the weather, so that there seemed no town but Garebridge, and nothing in that. It was the sort of melancholy that David enjoyed; but Keith was neither hungry at meals nor active between them. There was not even any preparation for school, because he had missed Friday afternoon, when the week-end's work was given out. It was always possible to go and find someone who knew what it was. But Keith felt, he thought, listless.

There were perpetual shadows at the edge of sight, too. He began to watch them, but it was hard to tell what he saw. It was as if some angles, and some darknesses, held pictures of the same army that had looked on him in the night. But now there were flashings of light in the shadows, and more sense of movement.

After breakfast he went upstairs and took a big glass of Liver Salts, because that was a treatment that often made him feel better. But this time it made no difference.

In the afternoon he went out to the shops, more for the sake of something to do than to buy anything. The whole town was busy with the Saturday folk who came to shop in their slightly detached way, as if they didn't belong to the town. The market place was full of cars, and the Cross was surrounded by buses. People walked umbrella'd and shining in raincoats, and the red buses shone in the road and glowed on the coats.

Then a car crossing the Square stopped with a swinging jerk, and there was the noise of tearing metal. Keith thought that another car had run into it from the other side. Then he saw the metal of this side was torn, and still bending, and the car was turned round with the weight of something pushing it, and Keith saw one of the things that had frightened the hounds and worried at the sheep. It was a blob, as high as a man, but with no proper shape, no colour, nor dimensions at all. It was more like a blister in the air, and it moved across the market place with the rain going through it as if it were not really there. Yet it was there, because it had moved through the front of a car. And now it moved against the flank of a bus that had stopped when the driver saw the first accident. It walked, or moved, down the hill, and as it came the cobbles below it were pressed into the ground, and stones cracked.

Others saw the ground being deformed, and looked

at the track that was being left. Only Keith saw the thing itself.

Last time it had meant lightning and David's death. What did it mean this time? It moved aimlessly, as if it were lost. Then it seemed to spin, and rise up, and was no longer there. As Keith turned to go home, frightened out of his shopping, the police came to sort out what had happened.

At home Frank Watson was taking off a wet coat and talking to Mr Heseltine.

'It's not that I mind paying,' he said, 'but it's the thought that counts, somehow, like Christmas presents. I don't like the thought. What are folk doing, sending in all manner of bills to be paid now, just like that, when they aren't due until next May Day? And folk aren't the same. It'll be cash, Mr Watson, all the way round, it'll be cash; and then that look they have, as if I'd been touched.'

Mr Heseltine was murmuring that he would sort it out, and Frank was interrupting him and saying he wanted a full showing, whatever that was. Then they went into the sitting-room, and began to talk properly.

Keith's mother explained better, when he went into the kitchen and dabbed at the chocolate cake that was mixing. 'Give up,' she said. 'That's all been weighed and measured. Folk don't like this boggart business. They think it'll be bad luck, and he'll go bank.' She used the local term for bankruptcy. 'If he did they wouldn't get their money, because no one would buy a farmhouse with a boggart in it, so there'd be no security. So they want their money now, instead of waiting, they think, for a part share. Well, that's put him about. Some of them think that, and the rest think he's mad.'

'What do you think?' said Keith.

'He's my cousin,' said his mother. 'And I'm descended

from the man who last had the boggart, and I think it's neither bad nor good. There's better sorts of creature to have in the house, and there's worse. So I wouldn't worry him for my money if he owed me any. And give up eating that mixture. It'll give you colic.'

That evening, after waiting to be struck by lightning since he had seen the thing in the market place, Keith went to bed early. He half thought the candle had called him, but he knew it hadn't. But when he went into his room he thought the light grew brighter. It was, in fact, bright enough to read by. He wrapped his dressing-gown round his already jacketed self, and sat at the table to read the notebook he and David had started to make. The candlelight was enough for him now, and he felt that he did not want to blaze a greater light on it.

He read what had been written, and wondered what to put next, hesitating over the choice of a sentence. Then, when he had a sentence ready he had to get up and find a pencil.

Downstairs the television throbbed. Up here there was no noise. The flame was still and silent, and the rain had stopped, leaving a still clear evening that might be frosty before the night was out. He licked the pencil, one end and then the other, sharp and flat, and laid the cold lead against his teeth.

There was a noise in the room. There was metal on metal. He looked round to see what it was, and there on the wall, or close against it, there was light, specks of it, like the reflection from a brass plate under a lacy doiley. The lights moved, not independently, but as if they were part of the same thing.

Keith thought he should feel frightened, but he wasn't. He looked with no more emotion than if he were watching television.

There was more than reflection now. There was shape,

in three dimensions, the shape of an arm, and the light was glittering on metal that clothed the arm, on links that shone in places, and were dull in others, as if the only cleaning they had had was the cleaning of use, and no metal polish or duster had touched them.

The arm lifted itself, like the arm that held Excalibur, only that had been clothed in white, and pointed, first with a hand that was not there, then with something longer, that grew into a sword. And that sword was, of course, Excalibur, and it was King Arthur that held it, pointing towards the candle. And with the movement of raising the arm came its sound, of heavy cloth rustling, and the metal of the lined armour sliding on itself. Then the sword tilted along its length, and flashed greeny-bronze, because it had a bright edge and a dull back.

Then the man himself stood there and looked at Keith, and moved his mouth. No words came, and then they did. And Keith could understand no syllable of it.

'Quis es?' said Keith, because his mind worked back as fast as it ever had to the Latin he had once done.

'Futurus sum,' said the figure by the wall, and looked again at the candle. And then he was not there, nor his sound, and the candle flickered, and revived again.

Keith picked it up. It was as heavy as lead.

3

THERE was something wrong, Keith thought. He should have been frightened by the unearthly figure, but he had not been. He had felt other things than frightened: sympathetic, for one, like the crowd at the inquest, not quite even curious about what was happening. He felt he was on the same side as the spectre that had come to him. And he knew, as well as he knew that yellow is yellow or blue is blue, that it was King Arthur. There was not even in him that little shiver down the back that he would have felt if an ordinary humble king, like the king of Greece today, or the king of Norway, had come into the room. He was equal to, or more powerful than, King Arthur, because the apparition had been asking him something. He did not know what.

He held the candle in his hands, and sat at the table still. The flame burnt steadily again, or more than steadily. There was weight to it now. The waxen part was as light as ever. It was the flame that was heavy, heavy in a strange way. If he lifted the candle up and down he felt ordinary weight, the kind that is a relationship between density, mass and gravity. But if he tried to move the candle about he felt a different sort of resistance, as if the flame was sticking to the space it was already in and did not want to move. He had to put his fist round the stalk and tug to move it about. He lifted it up to eye level, and let go. The candle stayed where he had put it, and did not fall to the ground as it should have done. He looked at it.

He was still looking an hour later, when his father came into the room and said 'What the devil are you doing, making that noise?'

The candle was still where he had put it. He looked away, and said that he was making no noise at all, and hadn't moved.

'No,' said Mr Heseltine, 'it isn't you. I'm sorry. It's out in the garden.' He went to the window and lifted it. Now Keith heard the noise. He went across the room and stood by his father.

'It sounds as if someone was sawing down the garden wall,' said Mr Heseltine. 'It must be the frost. I can see it sparkling everywhere. But I don't see how frost can make that sort of noise.'

Keith saw the lights too; but to him it was not reflections of frost. It was reflections on metal, on buckle and bridle and helmet, on the eye of man and the eye of horse: because outside there was arrayed the worn and unpolished army he had seen before.

He thought he had better make some sensible remark, since he knew without having to be told that his father had seen only frost. 'It'll be a tree branch against another one,' he said, 'swaying in the wind.'

'There isn't any wind,' said his father, closing the window.

'It'll be the station,' said Keith. 'That's what it will be.'

'Then I wish they wouldn't do their repairs at night,' said Mr Heseltine. 'Good night, Keith, don't leave that candle burning all night, strung up on cotton like that.' Then, having reasoned everything tidy he went to bed himself.

Keith opened the window again, and closed the collar of his dressing-gown against the cold air outside. He looked out on the army again. He tugged the candle over to the window and let its light flow out again.

He could see what the soldiers were doing, both footmen and horsemen. The horsemen were sharpening their green spears with stones, and turning a bright edge on the spearheads. Some were setting an edge on their swords, and one had a great axe with a curved blade, and he was cutting a crescent in that. And that was the noise that could be heard in the house.

Moving amongst them was King Arthur. His sword was in its scabbard, until he became aware of the candle, or of Keith. The sword came winking out then, and pointed to the candle, and the flame seemed to leap out and lick the bronze, but that was only an optical effect.

There was a murmur of voices, and then the men were on the backs of their horses, waiting for some word from

King Arthur. But he only looked at Keith and spoke words he did not understand.

Then his eyes searched for Keith's and held them. Now even the candle was invisible, and only the eyes of the king were in Keith's sight, looking into his. Keith began to know more than he had known. He began to understand that only he could touch the candle, and that he had to pick it up and take it somewhere. A picture came from eye to eye of a stone with a socket in it, somewhere underground. And from the back of his own mind he knew where that place must be: where the candle had come from in the beginning, when Nellie Jack John had brought it out into the world.

But what should he do now? His mind was filling with thoughts that were mere facts, not instructions. There was only the idea with them that something had to be done.

Then King Arthur turned away, and Keith felt his head move on his neck. He was falling asleep, because a great dizzy tiredness had come on him. He put his hands to his head, and the candle hung in air at the window, where he had put it. He walked backwards to his bed, and rolled on to it, pulled the bedclothes over him as he was, and slid, going backwards still, he thought, into an unilluminated depth of sleep that was as tempting as warm water to a tired body.

He woke hours later to a dark room, but not an empty one. He knew there was some company with him. He sat up, and suddenly realized that the candle was no longer there. Its light had gone, and it was not where he had left it, in the window.

There was light on the ceiling, coming in from the window, from some source low down in the garden. He got out of bed, and walked between visiting figures, who stepped aside for him, and looked out of the window.

The candle had sunk, and was now nearly on the ground below the window. Keith looked at himself, as if part of him could look at the other part, and saw that he was acting calmly, as if he knew what he was doing, as if he knew where he was going. The active part of him moved about the room, putting on shoes, and then out of the door. The observing part followed.

At the back door the two halves of him came together. He had been split by sleep, but now he knew that the whole boy was going to take the candle back to the place where it had come from, and should have done it before. It seemed such a simple thing to do. David should have done it: he had had the same visions, or in part the same visions.

In the garden there was the assembly of men, lined up now in some order of march, and ready to go, all watching the candle, but none able to touch it. Yet they would be able to touch it before long, if Keith did nothing about it. If they did touch it it would be wrong. It was not their time to handle it, and it never should be their time for it. Their time was to come, futurus sum, King Arthur had said; but perhaps the time never would be theirs to touch the candle.

When Arthur had first pointed at the candle, and Keith had touched it later, he had found it heavy, weighing some four and a half pounds. Now it weighed something like forty pounds, and it was more than he could support. Forty pounds is not an out-of-the-way weight. He could have man-handled a box weighing so much. But all the weight was concentrated in something three and a half inches tall and of the same circular size as a half crown piece, just over an inch and a quarter. To put his hand under it and lift was like being stood on. It tore at the flesh and warped his bones. In some ways it was like the handle of a very heavy suitcase, except that there was no swing to the heft of it: everything was in the palm of his hand.

He found a large plant pot, and scooped the candle up in that, and found he could lift it more readily, because the load spread itself better. He brought it up from the ground and held it to his chest.

When he turned from the lifting he found the column of horsemen was already moving, moving through the modern obstructions of wall and houses, on a line that was clear in the ancient days when they were alive. Because these were the knights of King Arthur, who slept with him under Garebridge Castle.

Some things they avoided. One house they stepped round, and in the market place they avoided something that was no longer there, so that Keith caught up where he had lost ground before.

He tried to go the way he wanted to go, along Hare Trod and the field called High Keld. But he was nudged back into the way the rest were going. Now the horsemen were becoming real, flesh against flesh, and he could smell the horses.

In a little while, as they were still in the market place, he found he was walking with ghosts no more, but with men, full and actual, casting shadows under the street lights, and sparks at their feet from the cobbles from the shod horses. Behind the company of horses were ranks of foot soldiers, coming up out of the dimness of the past into the solidity of the present, talking, singing, rattling weapons.

Keith was among them, as real as they were. People were waking in the houses round the market place, and looking out, and lights were being lit in rooms.

Then Keith found himself in Castle Wynd, with the Keep ahead, and the wrought iron gates that would, he thought, let spirits through, but not flesh and blood.

There was a noise ahead, and Keith saw the gatekeeper come out of his house and unlock the gates, and then stand aside. When Keith passed him, under the arch, with the light of dawn and the light of the candle to show him the man's face, he said Thank you to him. The man replied, 'It is the King,' and stood further into the wall. Keith saw that he was asleep. He wondered if he was.

The horsemen stopped on the sward inside the castle, bunched together as if they were enclosed within some no longer existent wall. Keith came in with them, and waited. Arthur came to him, took out his sword, and spoke. Keith did not know what he said, but followed when the King led him.

They threaded their way between obstructions no longer visible, and through an archway no longer there – the King bowed his head as he passed under it. They were on the edge of the rock, with the river far below, and beyond it the slope of the far side of the valley. On the skyline, where lightness filled the air, stood a row of huge stones, or giants. Keith was not sure which they were, but it did not matter, because standing stones were giants, and giants became standing stones whilst the King's time was standing still. And the King's time stood still when the candle Keith held was in its proper place under the ground, because King Arthur's time was not yet come. I know all this, said Keith to himself, feeling the words with his lips and yet not saying them aloud. I know that when Nellie Jack John took up this candle and brought it out from its place he disturbed the time that slept and the King that slept with it, and he woke what was asleep before, and things that have slept since, like the giants that had become standing stones, and the boggart; and the things that whirled. So there were giants in the old days, and they kept pigs, and there is nothing strange in their taking more pigs now that they are awake again.

And the wild boar had slept with them, perhaps like a stone too.

But what had taken David? What man riding had seized him and slain him and left nothing? Was that Arthur too? Keith looked round him. Here there was no crack in sky and ground, no opening to another time. Here there was no butterfly such as the one David had seen. There was only the brightening sky and the frosty earth and yonder hill fringed with giants, and the company of horsemen behind and around him, with the King leading, with his sword out, Excalibur with the dull green back and the sharp bronze edge that held light from everywhere, from star and morning and candle.

For the first time Keith suddenly felt afraid. He had come to the end of the knowledge that had been given him, and to the end of what he could imagine. There was no place here for the candle to be set, no rocky socket that it would fit, nowhere for the lock in time to be set again, and bind the King to the end of his sleep.

Then King Arthur leaned from his horse, pulled Keith up from the ground, held him under one arm, cried out, and sprang away down the hill, over some threshold of darkness in the rock, and dropped him again. Keith breathed out the strong smell of sweat and leather and regained his footing. Now, for the first time, he saw that he and the King were standing in the same plane, not at slightly different angles. Now they had come to their meeting place. And the King had his sword.

'Resurgam,' he said; and Keith knew that meant 'I will arise'; and that it should not be now. He looked round for the sky. But he was in a tunnel. The King pointed the sword, but not at the candle. It was pointing to Keith. Keith turned, and ran. He heard the horse beginning to move after him.

4

THERE was a shout behind, and the horse stumbled and scraped. Then there were more shouts, and Keith realized that the passage he was in was filling with horsemen. He hurried on, expecting at any moment to feel the sword Excalibur razoring through his clothes to his flesh and bone. Then he found he was ahead of the army. He had a light, they had none. And the light he had did not show behind him, because of the flower pot. He looked behind, but he should have known it was useless to do so. He did not turn the light round with him, and he could see nothing.

The noise grew. The ground underfoot grew rougher, but the walls began to spread. The candlelight shone on water and veins of crystal, and did not shine into the many fissures and crevices that textured the rock. He heard the hunt behind him spread to either side. Some of them seemed to have an easier road to tread, and were working up beside him.

Shortly he was no longer in a passage, but in a cave. The floor was littered with fallen rock; but with the light he had there was no difficulty in going forward at something like a run. The advantage of the candle was that it did not flicker in the hurrying air like a real candle.

The burden began to grow less. The candle was not so heavy. Instead of lying on the side of the tipped-over pot it began to roll about, a thing that did not affect the flame, but made it likely that he would drop the most helpful thing he had, and when he picked it up the followers would catch him. He held the candle in his hand. Then he threw the pot away. His mother would look for it, but that could be dealt with when the time came. If it did come: the followers had seen the naked light now, and were coming towards him with louder shouts. He thought he felt the warm breath of a horse at his neck.

He knew what had happened, and tried to shield the flame with his fingers. He had often touched this flame, and it was cold. But now it was no longer cold. It was warm. It was not yet so hot as flame, but it was not cold. He shielded the light, though, and hurried on. Overhead there was only shadow. To either side was shadow with glints of brass in it.

He came to a sandy place, an arena. At first he thought he was truly surrounded, and that the horsemen were waiting beyond the circle of light. Then he thought that the horses had been here before and left all the hoofmarks he saw. That was the right answer, he found, going on over the soft dry sand, because there was no horse there. But if he could go quickly on the sand the horses could go even more quickly, and he heard them begin to extend themselves, accelerating towards him.

His shoes rang on rock, and a table rose up like a little mountain in front of him, a little model mountain with a flat top. It was about ten feet across, and was circular, and in the middle was a little peak, a stone candlestick, empty. And that was where he knew he must put the candle.

He climbed on to the table, and as he did so there was a skidding thud behind him, and something brushed his heel, and a horse whinnied off into the dark and then wheeled. The horse had no rider. The rider was lying on the rock at the foot of the table, but getting up quickly. It was the King, King Arthur, who had leapt at Keith as he ran. He jumped up on the table beside Keith. Keith took the few steps that brought him to the middle, but he overshot, and had to turn. He held the candle firmly, and the flame began to scorch him.

There was a flash of light, reflected from Excalibur. The King had laid the sword over the socket, and was coming closer himself. Keith came forward at the same moment. The back of the sword did not look sharp, so he tried to push the blade away from that side of it. But the King brought the sword round suddenly and struck Keith with it. The cold bright edge sank into the upper part of his left arm. But at the same time, and before he felt the chill or the bite, the candle was in its place. And there was live wax on his fingers, because the candle was no longer a fossil of time, but purely existing in its own present.

There was sudden complete silence. Keith knew then that he was buried, far in the noiseless earth, and possibly further in the voiceless depths of time. The King stood without moving. Behind him stood the retinue that had been with him. And as Keith watched he saw each one shrouded in rock and grown with quartz, until they were stalactite and stalagmite and no more King Arthur and his Knights. Only the Round Table that Keith stood on gave any indication; and the candle standing alone.

Keith found he was not a stone, but himself, with a nasty deep wound in his arm, that was hurting very much, and bleeding a great deal. Blood was pouring from his sleeve and splashing on to the table. He gripped the arm, and the raw edges of the wound rubbed together, so that pain brought tears to his eyes and sobs to his throat.

He thought he was going to die, and he was about to sit down at the edge of the table and do so, when something else moved. He was frightened then, yet he thought it was silly to be frightened when you were dying of a wound in any case. But he slid down so that he might be hidden in the shadow of the table itself.

177

The thing he had seen moving came closer. Then Keith was up on his feet and forgetting wounds and fear and everything, because David was walking about in the sand, in his thoughtful way.

'Oh,' said David, when he saw Keith jump up. 'You've come, have you? I thought you wouldn't be long.'

'Wouldn't be long?' said Keith. 'How long have you been here?' The thought crossed his mind that he was dead too; but there seemed now to be a very big gap between a mortal wound and the state of death; so much that he wondered how mortal his wound was.

'I came about a minute ago,' said David. 'I was got here. Did you see how you were got here, because I didn't notice much?'

'I walked,' said Keith. 'Quick, how do we get out?'

'I haven't seen anything yet,' said David. 'Until you brought that candle. Where are we, anyway?'

'Under the castle, where Nellie Jack John was,' said Keith. 'That's why we'd better get out. Didn't you see King Arthur, or anyone?'

'I thought it was a butterfly,' said David. 'It grabbed me, and dragged me, and here I am.'

'David, David,' said Keith, 'you've been dead for months. You were killed by lightning on Hare Trod. Don't you know?'

But David was not listening any more. He was taking Keith's arm and looking at the blood that dripped black in the candlelight. 'We'd better go back,' he said. 'I expect the old man will put a stitch in that. You're bleeding like a pig.'

'Let's go then,' said Keith. 'I don't feel very well.'

It was one thing to want to go, but another to know where. They started at random, going on past the place where the table was, continuing in the way Keith would have gone if he had not stopped at the table. But without a light it was hard to know what to do. In a very little distance they found they were walking three- or four-legged, with hands as well, and had little idea what they were doing.

'I'll go and get that candle,' said David.

'Never,' said Keith. 'They aren't supposed to be out until it's finished burning, and it's going like a real candle now. We'd better hurry on as we are.'

They used the light, however, as a thing to walk away from. Then, a little to one side they saw another light, moving up and down very slowly, but not flickering. David guided Keith towards it, because Keith was feeling dizzy by now, and saw spinning lights where there were none at all.

The light was the light of an electric torch. It was the lamp from David's bicycle, and it was held by Nellie Jack John, who was walking at a snail's pace towards them. In relation to him they were racing by. Nellie Jack John looked as if he were working hard, and as if he were going very fast too. His hair, which was long below his cap, was streaming out behind him, and his clothes were pressed hard against him, and he was leaning forward. But the air round him was still.

'He's pushing against time,' said Keith. 'Try going back.'

David took a step back the way they had come. At once he found what Nellie Jack John was pushing against. He had once been on the back of a motor bike coming down Vendale. At a twisty humpy railway bridge the driver had put the brakes on firmly, and had slowed from eighty-five to twenty-five in the shortest possible space of time. David, hidden behind the driver, had felt the deceleration right through himself, as if the world were slowing down with him and becoming heavier with him.

'It's the weight,' he said. 'What shall we do with him?'

'He's been going a long time,' said Keith. 'There's hardly any light left in the torch.'

'It's being thinned out by time,' said David. 'That would be a natural effect. Shall we turn him round?'

So they turned him slowly round. One moment he was a dead weight in their hands, and the next he was running as fast as they could go, drumming violently, and sniffing at the same time.

'He's been all this time,' said David. 'Gosh.'

'We shouldn't have done it,' said Keith. 'It was wrong. He should have gone back the way he was going.'

'He never got there,' said David. 'You know he didn't. It would be better if he came with us, wouldn't it? It isn't an experiment any more. It's an actual event. I'm glad we came here. I'm glad we've turned him round. He can go and live with Frank Watson. We'll go straight up there and ask him and show him the boggart.'

'Oh, but you don't know,' said Keith. 'You don't know, David. You don't know everything that's happened.'

'Nothing's happened,' said David. 'But before we go to Swang we'll take your arm to the surgery. And you.'

'It might come off on its own yet,' said Keith.

There was light ahead of them, a very bright light, a strange radiance that reached into the tunnel they were in. Nellie Jack John looked round.

'I thowt there was other folk in wi' me,' he said. 'Where are we at now?'

They soon found where they were. The light was daylight, but the most cast-down leaden daylight Keith thought he had ever seen. It had only seemed bright after the darkness of the tunnel. It was cold too, because what gave radiance to the leaden light was snow.

They staggered out into High Keld into three feet of

snow, with more in the air, and a wind like a devil blowing. They could not see more than thirty yards.

'Thou's gitten nicked,' said Nellie Jack John. Red blood ran on the snow.

Keith wanted to sit down and gather his wits. David looked round in a dazed way, first at the snow, then at Keith.

'It's all wrong,' he said. 'It wasn't like this ten minutes ago. And how did you get a dressing-gown instead of a coat?'

'That's matterless,' said Nellie Jack John. 'He wants the surgeon, does that fellow. We'd best stop t'gab and tek him on.'

'I don't think it's an artery,' said David. 'I think it's just a cut. Help me on with him, Nellie Jack John.'

'It's so cold,' said Keith, and his teeth rattled against one another until he thought that they were moving sideways as well as up and down.

There was nothing to do but walk downhill, because downhill would bring them to the wall and the wall to the road, and the road to the town. It would not be easy to be lost.

So they came down, shivering, trembling, and came against the lights of the town.

'When is it?' said Keith. 'It might be any time.'

'It's not my time, then,' said Nellie Jack John.

'It's not mine,' said David. 'I never saw this snow before.'

'I can tell by yon lamp,' said Nellie Jack John, looking up at the street light. To David and Keith it looked enough like the one in the Wynd to be the same one. But to neither of them was the time of year, for one thing, the same as when they had gone in. And if it wasn't the time of year, then it might not be the same year of time either.

181

'Be ready,' said David. 'You've been with us before, Nellie Jack John. Stop now.'

Then they came to a familiar house, and a familiar lampshade in the room, and Keith fell down in a complete faint of weakness and pleasure that they were not far off their setting-out place. The house was Dr Wix's, and the lampshade the one in the study. He tried to tell David what had happened since that day on Hare Trod; but when he opened his mouth darkness came out of it, and he settled in the snow.

David opened the front door of the house, and he and Nellie Jack John lifted Keith inside.

5

DR WIX came out of the room where he was taking his solitary tea. He had heard the front door flung open and movement in the hall. What he found was a boy, lying wounded and bloody on the floor, the door wide open, and snow whirling in as far as the bottom of the stairs. Outside there was an array of footprints, but no one else in sight. He closed the door, turned back to the victim, and pulled him into the surgery and humped him on to the bench, being of the medical opinion that bones were not broken and there were probably no internal injuries. He tore away a sleeve of the dressing-gown and dropped it into the waste paper basket, cut off the sleeve of the shirt, saw the wound, and rang the police station, thinking of flick knives and gang warfare. The boy lay on his face. Dr Wix set to work to clean and stitch the wound.

When David and Nellie Jack John had lifted Keith into the house, Nellie Jack John had run out again at once, and gone away. David had run after him, and then for a time they were fighting in the snow. They were round the corner, and fought silently, on the counterpane of snow on the pavement, getting wet, but not in the least cold.

They were stopped by a policeman, hurrying down to Dr Wix's house to see what was the matter. He did not recognize David: no one would have, because he had a crew-cut of snow, and a jacket of the same, and there was blood on his face. Some of it was his own, from a wallop by Nellie Jack John, and some of it was Keith's. They were both out of breath and ready to stop, both on the point of giving up to the other. The policeman, who was Keith's friend, and perhaps should have known people even when they were disguised, took them under semi-arrest, and led them with him down to Dr Wix's house.

He was going to knock on the door, but David opened it and pushed Nellie Jack John inside first, then let the policeman in.

'He's in the surgery,' he said, hearing Dr Wix rattling a basin and running water. 'The waiting-room's there,' and he opened the waiting-room door to let the policeman in.

'I'll go straight in,' said the policeman. 'You wait here.' He had no doubt they would wait, because Nellie Jack John had sunk on to the floor, and appeared to be breathing his steamy last. The policeman went into the surgery.

'Come on,' said David to Nellie Jack John. 'We can't sit here.'

'I's jiggered,' said Nellie Jack John, letting go of his drum and the drumsticks. One of them had been broken in the fight. He tried to fit the pieces together, and then dropped them and shivered. David helped him up, and then took him upstairs. Nellie Jack John winced as the landing light went on. David took him into the bathroom and switched on the infra-red heater. Nellie Jack

John blinked round the little tiled room. David put the plug in the bath and ran hot water in.

'Get those clothes off,' he said. 'I'll find you some.'

'I'll have these to pay for,' said Nellie Jack John, looking at his ripped and scraped and soaked uniform.

'They'll be all right,' said David. Now, he thought, was not the time to make any points about elapsed time. He ran cold water in on the hot, and stirred it with the handle of the bath brush. Nellie Jack John sniffed at the soap, and undid buttons.

'It'll be better ner t'river,' he said. 'I've never been right in hot yet.'

Downstairs in the surgery the policeman had looked at the wound in the automatic unreacting way that policemen have. Then he had lifted Keith's head and looked at his face. It was covered in blood too. He took one of Dr Wix's swabs and wiped the blood off.

'Well,' he said, 'they shouldn't leave home. They only get in trouble. It's Keith Heseltine. Will he be all right?'

'Keith?' said Dr Wix. 'I wonder how he came by this nasty cut. It looks as if they were trying to take a steak out of him, whoever it was. But it's only a flesh wound, and I don't think there's any serious harm done. A nasty thing to come by. What will you do? Ring his parents?'

'In a moment,' said the policeman, Constable Hunter. 'There's two more lads in your hall now, got something to do with it, I shouldn't wonder. I'll bring 'em in, and we'll see whether they're hurt before doing anything else.'

Dr Wix covered Keith with a blanket and left him alone, and then followed the policeman to the door.

There was no one in the hall.

'They never went out,' said Constable Hunter. 'I had my eye on the front door all the time.'

'They'll have found the back door,' said Dr Wix. But he saw snow on the stairs, and they followed that track.

They found Nellie Jack John in the bath, with David scrubbing his back for him. Nellie Jack John stood up and hid behind a face flannel.

'I'd better explain who he is,' said David. 'It'll be a bit difficult.'

'Hmn,' said Dr Wix, with his mind baffled so that he could not think of the obvious thing, that this was David talking to him. His mind avoided the facts. Instead he looked at Nellie Jack John with a medical eye. 'That's a nasty rash,' he said, taking the face flannel away. 'I'll have a look at that by daylight. Does it irritate?'

'Does it what?' said Nellie Jack John, sitting down in the water and wrapping himself in his arms.

'Does it swidge?' said David.

'Who doesn't?' said Nellie Jack John.

'Here,' said Constable Hunter, 'I know one of these lads.' But it did not occur to him who David was.

'So do I,' said Dr Wix. 'I think.' Then he went to the mirror over the basin, wiped it clean with his hand, and looked at the pupils of his own eyes, to see whether he was normal or concussed or had done something that would alter his memory. He decided he was normal, and then felt a little thin and faint. He sat down on the nearest thing. 'It's David,' he said.

'We do know each other, actually,' said David. 'What about Keith? Is he all right?'

'Yes,' said Dr Wix. 'I've stitched him up. He's recovering on the couch.'

'Look, Doctor,' said Constable Hunter, 'there's more here than meets the eye. We'll go down again and wait for these two, and call Mr Heseltine.'

Before Dr Wix went down he looked closely at David, pinched his bare shoulder, and shook his head. He stood up, by habit turned the little lever on the cistern, and went out of the room. Nellie Jack John started away at the sound of gurgling water. David pushed him down and began on his neck with a brush. 'Tha's reet mucky,' he said.

When Nellie Jack John and David were clean and dry David found clothes for them both, stacked in the airing cupboard where they had lain since he disappeared. They went down, with Nellie Jack John suspicious of every strange thing. Dr Wix was in his sitting-room, with Keith in a chair opposite, still streaky with blood and very pale. Constable Hunter was sitting there too, with his helmet on his knees, drinking whisky with Dr Wix.

The door bell rang. Dr Wix went to the door and let in Mr and Mrs Heseltine. When they came into the room David and Nellie Jack John were sitting beside Constable Hunter, very pink and clean.

*

'The date's about October the twentieth,' said David, after a little time. 'But I don't understand about the snow.'

'The date is February the seventeenth,' said Constable Hunter. Then he named the year.

'Oh,' said David. But he was not very surprised. Keith had been more worried, because he knew how long David had been missing before he found him. There might have been a year, or a hundred years in it, or perhaps some awkward number like ten years. Now, or a long way off, were the best ones to be.

The next caller was Mr Wadham. Dr Wix had felt it necessary to call him, because he had after all declared David officially dead of lightning. He came in, twisted his yellow jaws, looked at David, put the jaw back in place, and said it was the first time he had spoken to a client after the event.

Frank Watson and his wife were stuck at Swang.

They could talk on the telephone, though, and long training with the boggart, that others would not believe in, made them able to understand without being too amazed. 'We could do with a lad,' said Frank. 'If he's without folk, like.'

'He's that,' said Dr Wix. Then he asked David whether Nellie Jack John knew about farming. Nellie Jack John said he was reared on a farm and could do owt, and his dad had taught him to salve sheep.

Frank Watson said there weren't many could do that these days, and he would dig out in the morning and come to see the lad.

'You're here now,' said David. 'And there's folk that want you, you'll have to stop.'

'Aye,' said Nellie Jack John. 'Is there any yal in t'spot?'

*

'One day you weren't there,' said Mrs Heseltine. 'And there was some trouble in the town during the night. People thought it was rowdies from the Hunt Ball, but it wasn't that night. There was a riot of some kind in the market place.'

'I was on duty,' said Constable Hunter. 'There was some sort of procession very early in the morning. I saw them myself. People had come to their windows to look, and shouted out to these men to be quiet. It's daft like, shouting to folk to keep quiet, you're liable to make more noise hushing them than they were making. But there was a few brickbats thrown, and windows broken, and a householder assaulted and rendered unconscious. But the offenders ran off into the Castle, and we didn't catch them. Then, next day, I wasn't on duty but I heard, there was a number a roads blocked with stones, big stones, like the Jingle Stones and that, bedded in the road. We made inquiries, and we found them all over the place, not just in roads, but stone circles where they weren't marked on the map. It was uncanny. Then, the next day, middle of the afternoon, and I observed it myself, there was upwards of three hundred pigs in the market place. It's daft, in a way, but no one saw them come in. One moment it was the market place, the next it was a pigsty. We rounded them up in the station yard, just in time to meet the four-fifteen. We weren't popular for a time. But they were the greater part of the missing pigs. And then there were stragglers, sows with little ones, in Finkle Street, and some in the cellars of the King's Arms, broken a barrel and drunk as lords, and singing, you never heard anything like it. But you know that fellow our vehicle ran down in Station Road. Well, all the pigs grew up the image of him, and it hasn't half upset the breeders. Then all's been quiet until tonight. However, we'll have a look in High Keld, when this lot's gone, and see what we can make of it.'

*

When the snow had gone Constable Hunter went to High Keld with David and Keith, and looked in the grass. It was unbroken. There was no trace of any opening. Constable Hunter said it was just as well, they didn't want other folk going in and getting lost; and if those inside wanted to get out, well, that was their affair, so long as they didn't break windows.

Nellie Jack John went to live at Swang. First, though, he had his hair cut, and instead of salving sheep, which had been given up thirty years ago, he himself was salved to get rid of his eighteenth-century rash. 'It was one of their big troubles in those days,' said Dr Wix. 'Skin diseases.'

The boggart became more and more idle, and by the end of the summer it had gone to sleep again under the bedroom floor. It would knock back if you knocked the board above it. 'It's just as well,' said Frank. 'It would wash the eggs, but it turned every one. I had to buy two dozen pot ones to keep it happy, and take them out and get them mucky for it. It was the only way. But we don't miss it so much now we have the lad.'

ABOUT THE AUTHOR

William Mayne was born in Hull in 1928, the son of a doctor, and lived for many years with his three sisters and brother in a small house on the edge of a moor in Yorkshire.

From 1937 to 1942 he attended the Canterbury Cathedral Choir School. He says that his formal education ended in 1945, when he resolved to make writing his career. His first book was written during the summer holidays, when he was sixteen. He gave it to a little girl he knew and never tried to publish it.

His first book, *Follow the Footprints*, was published in 1953. His early work attracted immediate attention, but the book that secured him recognition as a brilliant writer for children was *A Swarm in May*, a story set in a cathedral choir school that can only be Canterbury. This book, together with its successors *The Member For The Marsh* and *Choristers' Cake*, appeared on the lists of runners-up for the Carnegie Medal. It was *A Grass Rope*, which, like a number of his other books, has a Yorkshire setting, that won him the Medal itself for 1957.

He has written many books since then, including *A Parcel of Trees*, *Pig in the Middle*, *No More School*, *The Battlefield*, *Sand*, and *A Book of Giants*, all of which appear in Puffins.

William Mayne is unmarried and lives in Yorkshire. The whole of his adult life has been given up to writing for children, with the exception of a very brief (one term only) spell of schoolmastering. He is interested in music and has composed a little. He is also interested in vintage cars and loves engines and mechanical things.

if you have enjoyed this book and would like to know about others which we publish, why not join the Puffin Club? You will receive the club magazine, *Puffin Post*, four times a year and a smart badge and membership book. You will also be able to enter all the competitions. Write for an application form to:

The Puffin Club Secretary
Penguin Books Limited
Bath Road
Harmondsworth
Middlesex